The Bizarre Events at Hellman Elementary

Jurassic Field Trip

Bentley,

Keep it strange!

Richard M. Born

Richard M. Born

PAGE PUBLISHING, INC.
New York, NY

First originally published by Page Publishing, Inc. 2018

ISBN 978-1-64350-028-7 (Paperback)
ISBN 978-1-64350-029-4 (Digital)

Printed in the United States of America

For Luke. Be whatever you desire. Daddy will always love you.

The September air was hot even though the sun had set hours ago. Dylan ran through the jungle as fast as he could. He could feel beads of sweat rolling down his nose. He knew this whole thing had been a bad idea. How many laws had he actually broken just by breaking into the place? If he got out of this mess, maybe he would go to jail. A dreadful feeling came over him; jail time was the least of his worries. Just getting out alive was his main goal at the moment.

Dylan listened closely for the sound of the guards. Had he lost them? He looked around. How do I get out of this place? He could see a small path up ahead through some fallen brush. If he could make it to the path, he could figure out how to get to the front entrance and get out of here without being caught.

Just as he started to head toward the path, a pair of shoes came into view. "I see him, he's in the west jungle," the guard roared. "Mr. B ain't gonna like it if the little squirt gets away!"

Dylan dove to the right, deeper into the trees. The vines had grown thicker and had spread like strange spider webs across the earth. He was going farther away from the only hope of escape. His heart was pounding in his chest; he was afraid that at any moment it was going to burst out of his chest. He didn't dare to look back; he had long legs but the guards were still faster. Any second now, they would be right behind him. Suddenly the ground sloped downward; it felt like one of those old cartoons where the coyote stands in midair until he looks down to see that there is no ground beneath him. Dylan tumbled and rolled down the sloping hill. As the ground leveled out, he came to an abrupt halt, hitting a mound of mud with the back of his head.

He lay dazed for a few moments looking up at the star-filled sky. He appreciated how beautiful it was and thought it funny that he had never taken the time to see how wonderful life is. How was it that he had gotten himself into this? He was never going to get out of here. All this for a girl that he would never see again, and he was going to die before he could get his first kiss. This thought brought up even more bad feelings. He would never reach the fifth grade, never get a driver's license, never see his grandma again. He had wanted to impress Paige, show her how brave he was, but he wasn't feeling very brave covered in dirt and muck. He tried to lift his head, pain shot through it, but he slowly got to his feet.

"Over there! He went that way," yelled a guard. Dylan looked around; he didn't know this part of the park. It looked as if he had fallen into the restricted zone. Another rule broken. He sighed. Even worse was that he had no clue how to get back to the main gate from here. He looked up the hill; he must have fallen at least a half of a mile. If he tried going back up he would run directly into those guards, but who knew what would happen to him if he went deeper into the jungle.

He could see the beams of flashlights sliding through the trees at the top of the hill. He had to make a decision now; maybe they would just ban him from ever returning to the park. That would be the best scenario, but he knew that it would not go down that way because he knew too much. His head was still pounding as he launched himself deeper into the unknown. His legs were getting weak. How long had he been running now? It felt like hours. Then his foot slammed down into a black puddle of mud. He lost his balance and once again found himself falling into the muck. He got to his knees, and pulled at his foot but it was in too deep. There was a noise from somewhere to his right.

"I'm positive he came this way. I can smell him," said a rough voice. "This is Slayer's territory. I would not go into this part in the day time much less in the dark," came a second voice. Even though he could not see who was speaking, he recognized the voices of the two head guards. He stayed very still, scared that his hammering heart would give him away as he tried to hold his breath.

They had to be only a foot away. "I can definitely smell him. My sense of smell has never been wrong. He came this way. He couldn't have gotten very far in the dark," the guard with the rough voice exclaimed.

"We won't get very far either if we go into that area," responded the second guard. "We should head back and inform Mr. B of the situation. Besides, if he did run into the area, he will head straight to certain death. Slayer doesn't like visitors."

The other guard sounded concerned. "Mr. B is not going to like the fact that we let him get this far and then lost him. Let's go. Maybe he won't punish us if we tell him how sorry we are for letting the little brat get killed in the restricted zone."

The two guards slowly started walking back the way they had come. Dylan let out a deep breath. "That was close," he thought. Maybe there was a little bit of hope. Then it occurred to him that they didn't want to be in this area. "Why not?" he asked himself. Who was this Slayer that they were scared of? Oh well, now was not the time to be worried about that; he needed to get out of here. As he stood up, he realized that something was wrong. While he had been standing still listening to the guards talking, he had not noticed that his feet had been sinking deeper into the mud.

He started to panic; the mud was up over his knees! He tried to lift his leg but found that he could not move it even an inch and the more he tried, the faster he sank. "What kind of mud is this?" he whispered. He started to try to dig his legs out; the mud had risen almost to his waist. As he put his hand into the mud, he discovered that it had a strange smell. Why had he not smelled it sooner? Panic really washed over him now. He was not sinking into mud. It was tar and he was trapped. There was no escape! The secret that he had learned would die here in this tar pit with him. The tar was up to his chest now and he could barely move. He stretched out his neck and gasped for air as the tar continued to rise. It almost felt as if a hand was pulling him under faster and faster. He thought of his best friend JP As the tar reached his mouth, he knew that he would become one of JP's strange stories about their elementary school, Hellman Elementary. Dylan closed his eyes as the tar sucked him down.

Four days earlier

Beep . . . Beep . . . Beep . . . Dylan pulled the heavy comforter off his head and reached for the snooze button on his alarm for the fifth time that morning. He missed with a clatter as the alarm clock hit the floor. Trying to still stay halfway under his covers, he reached down to grab the clock. As his hand felt for the plug, an older woman opened his bedroom door.

"Dylan, sweetheart, it's time to get up and get to school. You don't want to be late," said his grandmother softly.

"Yes, I do." Dylan replied groggily. "Why do I even have to go to school?"

His grandma carefully walked over to the bedroom window, trying not to step on the controller and video games that had not been put back into their cases. She pulled on the window shade and it quickly rolled up with a loud snap. The sun was just starting to rise and was shining directly on Dylan's face.

"Ah, too bright," he said, pulling the covers up over his head again.

"I see that you were up late again playing video games." His grandma sighed as she turned off the TV. "You need to get a move on. You don't want me to have to drive you to school, do you?" she said with a slight grin. "I don't know, maybe it would do me good to get out for a bit. I could throw on my bright green robe, and my pink house slippers. It would be nice to walk you in for a change. I haven't walked you in since you were in first grade." She knew that this would get him up and moving. "I could eat breakfast with you and your friends."

"I'm getting up. I am a big boy now in the fourth grade and I don't need you to walk me into school," Dylan replied, throwing his legs off the bed to stand up. As he stretched his arms into the air, his pajama shirt rose to reveal his outie belly button.

"You are getting much too tall for that dinosaur pajama shirt, so maybe it's time to pass it down to your brother," said his grandmother as she gently kissed his cheek. "Don't forget your PE uniform."

Here was another good reason to skip school. He hated PE. It wasn't that he disliked the exercises; it was the plain and simple fact that the PE coach, Coach Sara, was a total lunatic. She hated kids in general and she did not even try to hide the fact. Just last month she had caused him to fall from the top of the gym ceiling as he was climbing up the rope. "You know if you loved me you would let me stay home. I could stay home and help you clean the house," he said with a toothy grin.

"You help with the cleaning?" His grandmother laughed, picking up dirty dishes from under his bed. "Also, I want you to make sure that Caleb gets to school all right."

"Please tell me you're joking," Dylan said, getting annoyed. "He's a pain in the ass."

"Watch your language young man, or I will wash your mouth like I wash your underpants," his grandmother replied. "Now hurry up and get dressed. I will get your backpack ready." She walked out of the room. As she pulled the door shut, it snagged on a pair of his jeans. "And when you get home today, I want this room cleaned up."

As she walked out, Dylan looked around the room. It didn't look that bad, he thought. He quickly pulled on the jeans that had snagged under the door. His room looked like any other ten-year-old's. "It is organized chaos," he thought as he shoved old toys under his king-size bed, reaching for a pair of socks. The room was a little cramped because of his bed, but he needed the large bed due to his long legs. Long legs were a staple in the Rook family tree. His mother, aunts, cousins, and brother had long, spindly legs.

His grandfather had stood almost eight feet tall. He had passed away last year. It was tough on the family, and whenever he was mentioned, his grandmother would have to go use the restroom. Dylan and his brother had lived with his grandparents for seven years. Their father had some issues with Caleb and left town. He didn't much like his little brother either, but he never understood why their father left. Caleb was different from most other kids; he still believed in fairy tales and talked to invisible people. His favorite thing to do was to make my life a living nightmare.

Furthermore, over the summer, I had my first ever boy-and-girl birthday party. I had asked my grandma if he could go stay with Aunt Sally, but she didn't want her two perfect sons to be around a wacko even if it was her nephew. At first, I thought that he would be nice and content playing my PS3 in my bedroom. Boy, was that a mistake! He spilled lemonade on my bedsheets and brought them to my grandmother in front of everyone and told that I had wet my bed. Everyone laughed at me.

To make matters even worse, when it came time to open my presents, he came downstairs with a sheet tied around his neck and just his underwear. He yelled the he was a super villain and jumped onto my presents. And what he did to the cake, I won't even talk about.

Dylan finished pulling on his sneakers and left the room to grab some breakfast before he headed to school. He started walking down the hallway; it was eerily silent as he went towards the kitchen. As he passed his mom's bedroom door, he froze. There in the dark were a pair of red eyes looking straight at him. Dylan walked a little closer to the door and the eyes blinked. Dylan screamed as the creature jumped!

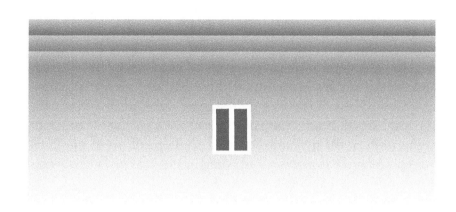

The creature jumped from the bed, and Dylan felt his feet slide out from beneath him as he backed toward the door. His head hit the floor with a loud thud. The creature was standing over him; its face was swimming in front of Dylan. Dylan rubbed his eyes trying to get them to focus. The monster's teeth were yellowed and the skin was torn on its face looking like it had been stitched up badly. Dylan started crawling toward the door. As he did so, he got a better look at his attacker.

The monster was standing on two tall legs, wearing an old pair of jeans and a blue T-shirt. It bent down into Dylan's face and yelled "Gotcha! You should have seen your face." Caleb took off the mask, and his dirty blond hair fell over his large ears. Still laughing, he made a face of fear. "I wish I had a camera."

Dylan pulled himself up against the doorframe. "You should put the mask back on; it was an improvement. It covered up your elf ears." He knew he had hit a sore spot. Caleb hated his ears as they were abnormally large and pointy at the top. Normally, he kept his hair over them so that people would not see.

Caleb's face turned bright red. "I'm telling Grandmother that you are making fun of me!" He threw the mask onto the bed and ran out of the room.

"What a sniveling little brat," Dylan said aloud. He walked into his mom's room; no one was supposed to come into this room.

Even though his mom had not stayed here in over a year, she used the room to store her notes on things that she had dug up. The room had a musty smell. Grandmother hardly ever came in here to clean. She never saw eye to eye with Dylan's mom. She did not understand why his mom always chose her job over her children. Dylan walked over to his mom's dresser; he looked at all the pictures. She had been all around the world. There was a picture of her standing in front of the pyramids in Egypt, and one of her at the Eiffel Tower. The most recent one had come in the mail just a few weeks ago showing her standing by a baby kangaroo.

Dylan picked up the picture to take a closer look at it. In the picture, she had a big smile on her face as she fed a bottle to the baby. It was the only time that he could see her smile. She was never happy while she was home as she and Grandpa were always butting heads. She didn't even come home for his funeral. Even when she did come home it would only be for a day or two. She always had an excuse as to why she couldn't stay longer; she didn't even send a birthday card this past year.

"She must really love her job." Dylan sighed as he put the photo down. He looked at the picture from Egypt, his mom's long purple hair blowing behind her, making her look as if she were a model. The sun glistened off her nose rings. Like in all the other pictures, she had a wide smile showing her beautiful white teeth. He ran his hand over the top of the dusty dresser, leaving a strip of cleanness in the dust. He turned to her closet; Caleb must have been messing around in there because the door was open.

He walked toward the closet to shut it, looking in to see if his brother had moved anything. His mom didn't keep many clothes in here, mainly just her wedding dress which she had hated. She hardly ever wore anything other than camo shorts and rock band T-shirts. As his hand touched the doorknob, he felt a breeze. He shut the door and focused his attention on the window; he didn't even realize that the window hidden behind the open closet door could be opened.

He looked at the drawn shade. Maybe it was his imagination, but he thought he saw a shadow. An eerie feeling came over him, and he could feel the hair on the back of his neck stand up. It looked as if there was a person standing right outside the window. It felt like someone was watching him from the other side of the window. He shut the closet and reached his hand toward the drawstring of the window shade. He pulled hard and . . .

"Dylan! You need to hurry up! Your breakfast is getting cold!" came his grandmother's voice from downstairs.

He jumped as the shade shot upward. Nothing was there; the window was opened just a crack so that must have been how he felt the breeze. "Be there in a minute," he yelled not taking his eyes off the window. Walking over to the window, he looked outside. No one was in his backyard. He pushed the window closed and turned the old lock at the top making sure that it was good and latched. There was a strange smell in the air, a familiar smell; he stood at the window for a moment. He had smelled it before, but he couldn't think of where.

Turning to the bed, he picked up the mask that his brother had left behind. "It was just the shock of the mask," he thought to himself, "that's why I'm so jumpy." Dylan noticed the mask had been covering up a small wooden box that he had never seen before. "Dylan, you are going to be late if you don't put some pep in your step," hollered his grandma. Picking up the box, he turned to go downstairs. When he got to the door, he stopped and turned back to the window. He pulled down the shade and checked the room once over, then headed off to the kitchen. He didn't even notice that there was no longer a shadow at the window.

He jumped the stairs two at a time, grabbed his backpack from the hook on the hallway door, and entered the kitchen. His brother was sitting in a yellow chair eating a plate of bacon. "You took too long. I just ate the last strip of bacon. You can have the eggs," said Caleb.

"I hate eggs," Dylan said, grabbing a slice of toast. "And I hope you enjoyed the bacon. I don't eat it. Bacon makes your ears grow super fast." He laughed.

"He's making fun of me again, Grandma!" Caleb exclaimed.

His grandma gave him a dirty look. "Knock it off, Dylan. You know how your brother gets." She was standing at the stove frying a couple of eggs. "Now you need a healthy breakfast to get your day going," she said as she put the two eggs on the plate.

"I truly hate eggs," he thought, taking the plate out of her hands. He sat down at the table across from Caleb.

"Have you seen Bonedigger this morning?" asked Caleb. "He was sleeping with me last night but got up at exactly four fifty-three. I thought he was going to use the bathroom, but he never came back."

Bonedigger was the family's pit bull. He was a present from Dylan's dad. Dylan shook his head. "I have not seen him yet." Which was a bit odd; they had Bonedigger since he was a puppy, and every morning he would greet Dylan in the kitchen before he left for school.

"Bonedigger!" he yelled. He listened for the dog to bark, but there was nothing. "Bonedigger!" he yelled once more. "Grandma, have you seen Bonedigger?"

His grandmother sat in the chair next to him. "The last time I saw him, he was chewing on your grandfather's shoes, but that was yesterday." She poured herself a glass of orange juice. "Now don't get your undies in a twist. I'm sure he will show up, probably with a squirrel for me to chase out of the house again."

Caleb laughed. "Yeah, I remember the last time he brought a raccoon in to play with."

Dylan gave a small smile; he too remembered the event. Bonedigger was about sixty pounds of muscle. If you didn't know him, you would probably run away in terror, but he really was a big teddy bear and would not hurt a fly. He loves making friends; he had caught the raccoon in hopes the he could play with him. Grandma didn't find it funny at all; Bonedigger had put the raccoon on her bed, then played a game of hide and seek with him. Pit bulls get a bad rep; Bonedigger was the friendliest dog ever.

"Bonedigger!" Caleb screamed, jumping to his feet. "I am worried. What if he is hurt?" Tears started to appear in his eyes.

Dylan felt a little sorry for his brother. He loved Bonedigger; it was kind of like having someone that he could talk to. He knew this because during stormy nights, he could hear Caleb talking through the vents. He talked to the dog as if it were his mother. There was a loud crash at the front door, then the doorbell rang.

His grandmother stood up. "Who could that be this early in the morning?" She left the kitchen. Dylan could hear her opening the front door. There was a loud bark as Bonedigger ran into the room. He jumped up and started licking Dylan's face. Caleb, looking relieved, came and gave the dog a big hug. But the dog could not have rung the doorbell, Dylan thought. Who had been at the door?

His question was answered almost immediately. His grandmother was walking back into the kitchen, and following her was a skinny, geeky-looking boy. Terry was thanking his grandmother for letting him come in. "If I hadn't run into Bonedigger, I would have been dead meat for sure."

Terry was Dylan's next-door neighbor. Like Dylan, Terry lived with someone other than his parents. In Terry's case, he lived with his great aunt, Margie. She and Grandmother had been friends for years. He was in the fourth grade and in the same class as Dylan. He was extremely nerdy, and his name did not help matters, as it was Terry Dactyl. Lots of people made fun of his name. Unlike Dylan, Terry was short for his age; the way he hunched his back made him look even smaller.

Terry never mentioned his birth parents, so Dylan didn't know much about them, only that they left him with his aunt at the age of three. He was strange. As a little boy, he didn't know how to speak very well and still had a lisp. His aunt spent a lot of money on doctors, but Dylan was not quite sure why.

Terry ran his hand over his buzz-cut hair. "Hey, Dylan," he said breathlessly, "Josh and his buddies were chasing me again."

Dylan noticed how dirty Terry's face looked. He got up and got a washcloth from the sink and handed it to him. "You shouldn't let those jerks get to you. They are just upset that you get straight A's and they are still in elementary school." Terry wiped his face and Dylan noticed how pointy his nose was. "Do you want to ride with me and Caleb to school?"

"Yeah, that would be great." Terry grinned. "You are always nice to me."

"Well, you three better get going," Grandmother said while helping Caleb get his backpack on. "You don't want to miss the morning announcements."

Getting up and putting on his backpack, Dylan replied, "Yeah, we would not want to miss that." He rolled his eyes and slid the two uneaten eggs into Bonedigger's bowl, which the dog slurped down very quickly. "We can go out the back. We need our bikes," he said to Terry.

They left the kitchen and walked out into the warm day. Dylan and Caleb got on their bikes and rode into the front yard so that Terry could get his; there were no signs of Josh. They started to ride; the school was about a ten-minute bike trip. Dylan enjoyed riding his bike as he could feel the wind blowing through his hair. They turned the street corner and he could see the school ahead. It looked dreary and unwelcoming. "You know they should really spend some money and repair the school," he said to Terry. "I bet that the school has not had a paint job since it was built."

Terry turned his head to comment. In the split second that he did not pay attention to the road, he hit a rock. Terry went flying into the unmowed grass as his bike collided with the steps of the school.

"Wow, I thought pterodactyls could fly." An African American boy laughed, standing next to Terry's side. He was wearing a black shirt with jeans. Flexing his arms, he walked closer to Terry, who was getting to his feet.

"Knock it off, Josh," Dylan said as he stopped his bike and started to lock it to the bike rack in front of the school. "Just leave him alone." Josh was not an easy kid to get along with. Most of the kids at the school were afraid of him. He was in fifth grade for the third time. Dylan didn't care; he was not going to go through life being afraid of a bully. "So, Josh, do you think you might pass this year or are you just staying because you love the food?"

Josh snarled at Dylan, "You had better watch your back!" He shoved Terry back to the ground and walked into the school. "Geek!"

"The J shaved into his hair should stand for jerk not Josh," said Dylan as he helped Terry up. "Caleb, you better go on to class. I will lock up your bike. And remember to meet me here after school."

Caleb nodded and ran off and into the school. Dylan helped Terry lock up his bike. "Do you want to ride home with us this afternoon?"

Dusting off his knees, Terry replied, "I have a dentist appointment this afternoon." Terry frowned. "I hate the dentist. You want to come with me?" They started walking up the dirty concrete stairs.

"Can't. I promised to clean my room this afternoon." Dylan opened the door. "Well, guess I'll see you later." He turned and headed to the gym for morning announcements.

Dylan walked into the gym, searching for some of his friends. Looking around the bleachers, he saw his friend JP and went to sit with him. JP was a skinny boy, but lately it seemed as if he had stopped eating, and he had these green eyes that seemed to look deep into your soul. Most of the kids at the school took pity on him because his older brother had disappeared two years ago. No one really knew what happened to him. Most kids said he ran away, while others said that his parents sent him to military school. JP didn't believe either; he says that the school somehow got him.

Dylan admitted that there were some pretty strange things about Hellman Elementary, but JP took it way too far. He even stopped going to the bathroom last week because he said there was a seaweed monster in the sewers. Crazy, right? He had made it his life's mission to discover all the school's secrets.

"You look like you didn't sleep much," Dylan said as he sat down. "Are you going on the field trip tomorrow?"

"I haven't slept well in a week. I keep having bad nightmares. Yeah, the field trip sounds fun," said JP in a tired voice. "Did you get your math homework done?"

Dylan hit himself on the head. "No, I totally forgot about it. Let me copy yours?" JP pulled a sheet of paper out of his bag and handed it to Dylan. Dylan took out his homework sheet from a folder inside his bag. He grabbed his pencil and quickly started copying the answers down. As he crammed his completed homework back into his bag, he noticed the wooden box he had taken from his mom's room. He pulled it out and began to inspect it closer.

"What's that?" asked JP.

Dylan turned the box over in his hands. "Not sure," he replied. "I found it in my mom's room this morning. I thought it was a box but I can't figure out how to open it." The box looked very old and had pictures carved into the wood. Maybe his mom had bought it just for decoration.

"Here, let me take a look," JP said, taking the box out of his hand. "Interesting, the pictures are hand-carved. Would you care if I borrowed this? I can get it cleaned up during lunch. Then we could see the pictures better."

Dylan didn't like the idea of letting his mom's things go with someone else, but JP was good at mysteries. "I guess so, but please be careful with it."

"Awesome," said JP as he slid the box into his bag. "I won't let anything happen to it."

It was almost time for school to start. Any minute now, Principal Schmitt would walk out and start giving the morning announcements. Dylan noticed that the bleachers had started to fill up around them. A boy named Samuel Villias came to sit with them.

"What's up, guys?" he said, moving his LL Bean backpack in front of him. "I could hardly wait to get to school today. Guess what I got for my birthday." He reached into the front of his bag and pulled out a baseball card.

"It's a Babe Ruth and it's autographed!" Samuel said with excitement.

Dylan liked Samuel; they had been friends since kindergarten, but he was a little jealous of him as well. Samuel, who went by Sam, always had a cool attitude about him. He was perfect. He had good grades and good looks, and all the girls liked him. He wore jeans that seemed to fit perfectly and T-shirts that seemed to show off his six-pack. He was more of an outdoor kid than Dylan. Sam was on every sports team that Golfing Blue had to offer. He lives and breathes sports. Dylan would prefer to stay inside and watch a game on TV. Sam was even on the cover of Golfing Blue's sports magazine.

"So what did you think about that math homework?" Sam asked, sweeping his fingers through his bangs so that his hair looked windswept. "It took me about five minutes. I even did the two bonus problems." He smiled and Dylan noticed his perfectly white teeth.

"Oh yeah, easy as pie," said Dylan, glancing at JP and grinning.

The gym door opened once again and Paige Tilton walked in. It was like the air had been sucked out of the room. Dylan watched as her long curly blond hair bounced on her shoulders as she walked to the bleachers. Her green eyes searched for her friends. She sat down just a couple of rows in front of the three boys. Dylan could smell her strawberry hand lotion. He had been in love with her since the first day of school. Paige was a very popular girl and a lot of boys had a crush on her, including Sam.

"I'm gonna go show Paige my birthday gift," Sam said with a smile. "That is unless you have an issue with that?" he looked at Dylan.

"No, go right ahead," Dylan said, looking at his shoes. He could feel his face heating up. "She would like you better anyway."

"You've got to have some confidence," Sam replied. He stood up and hopped down a couple of seats. "Paige, check it out," he said, showing her the card.

Dylan watched as she smiled. She had a beautiful smile. "That's so cool, Sam. Maybe I can come watch your next baseball game," she giggled.

Sam looked up at Dylan, then turned back to face her, "You know I'm going to have a birthday party in a few weeks. You want to come?"

Paige gave a quick glance in Dylan's direction. He tried not to notice. "I thought your birthday was yesterday," she replied.

Sam ran his fingers through his hair again. "Yeah, but I could not have my party because my parents were busy, so they said I can have one in a couple of weeks. It's going to be real fun!"

Dylan didn't want to hear any more, so he turned his attention to JP, who had pulled out the little wooden box again. "So you think that those pictures mean anything?"

JP looked up. "I think I have seen something like this before. I just can't remember where." Suddenly the room got very quiet. Even though the gym had no air conditioning, Dylan felt chilled.

"Quick, put it away," Dylan said as a woman dressed in black walked into the gym.

Principal Schmitt was always the one who gave the morning announcements. "*Quiet!*" she said, but she really didn't need to at that moment because you could have heard a pin drop. Her wispy gray hair was up in her usual bun. Nobody wanted to get on her bad side. Dylan looked over at the third graders. He saw Caleb, and he was patting an invisible person's back. He looked back at the principal. She began talking. "Good morning." Her voice was loud and crisp. "I hope we are all ready to get the day started. If you are a bus rider this afternoon, bus 66 had an unfortunate accident yesterday. We are very happy no one was badly injured. However, the bus will need to be repaired. So if you normally ride bus 66, today you will ride on bus 6. Don't miss it. I hear it will be a fun ride."

Dylan noticed Sam whispering something to Paige. It gave him an uneasy feeling in his stomach. He returned his attention to Mrs. Schmitt. "Mr. Jibby has informed me that the lockers in the fifth grade hall have been slamming shut on students. Should you find yourself locked in your locker, scream for him and he will move the locker to an empty room."

She gave an evil smirk. "That concludes this morning's announcements. Kindergarten to second, you are dismissed. Third to fifth, please stay seated."

Dylan watched as the younger kids left the gym. Sam came back to sit next to Dylan. "I just asked Paige if she wanted to be my bus buddy for the field trip, and she said yes."

Dylan felt butterflies in his stomach. "Good for you."

The last of the younger children had left the gym. The principal looked stern as she addressed the upper grades. "As you all are aware, tomorrow is our field trip to Dino Kingdom. I expect the very best behavior. If you put a toe out of line, do not expect to have feet when you return to school." Everyone was silent. They all knew she meant business.

"The buses will leave at 8:00 a.m. sharp. If you miss the bus, then you will write a one-hundred-page essay on why you were late. If you will not be attending our lovely trip, then you will be staying with fifth grade teacher Dr. Bates, who says it is too hot for him to go to Dino Kingdom. He will have a list of students. If you are on the list and do not show up for school, then you will be in my office Monday morning." Once again, an evil grin spread across her face. "Now, get to class, all of you."

Principal Schmitt walked out of the gym. The students were standing up and making their way toward the gym door. Sam grabbed his bag. "Let's go through the cafeteria. It will be quicker," he said. Dylan and JP grabbed up their bags and headed toward the cafeteria doors. A few other students had the same idea.

They started to slowly move past the kids in the cafeteria. Dylan was still a little jealous of Sam. "What was so much better about Sam?" he thought. He was walking to Sam's left side, and JP was a couple of steps in front of them. "JP, zip up your bag," Dylan said. "I don't want anyone to see that box."

JP stopped and zipped his bag up. "I won't let anything happen to it. I promise."

Sam looked puzzled. "What is this secret box?"

Dylan considered not telling Sam, but they had been friends forever. "I found this strange box in my mom's room."

A look of excitement came over Sam's face. "Way cool! Maybe it's something she found on one of her expeditions. What is in it?"

Dylan shook his head. "I'm not even sure how to open it. JP is going to get it cleaned up at lunch."

A glassy look came over Sam's eyes. "What if there is treasure inside?" His eyes came back into focus. "Or what if it is cursed?"

Dylan laughed. "A curse?! Don't be ridiculous! There are no such things."

JP gave him a look. "I wouldn't be so sure. This is Hellman Elementary, home of the weird."

Dylan rolled his eyes. They walked on. Dylan stopped and sniffed the air. He smelled the same scent that he smelled in his house. Suddenly, he felt a hand hit his arm. He turned in time to see Sam slam to the ground and roll right in front of the big trashcan.

To most, this might not have seemed like a big deal, but what lived behind the trashcan had also seen Sam fall. It was heading right for Sam. Dylan saw the look of terror on his friend's face as the huge spider had wrapped his ankle in webbing. Sam was about to be a fly for the spider's lunch.

Sam!" yelled Dylan. "Help, grab his arms, JP!" Dylan and JP grabbed Sam's arms. The spider was strong. Dylan could see the spider's hairy pinchers and eight milky white eyes.

"Please help." Sam's face looked as if it were in pain. The spider's pinchers were getting closer. If Sam was dragged behind the trashcan, there would be no saving him. JP lost his grip and let go of Sam's arm. Dylan, losing his balance, stumbled a few feet but held tight to Sam's arm.

"I'm not going to let go." Dylan could see tears running down Sam's cheeks. He may have been a little jealous that Sam got the girl, but he didn't want him to die, thought Dylan whose face had beads of sweat rolling down. With a burst of strength, he turned Sam onto his back and got a better grip under his armpits. He pulled as hard as he could but it still was not enough. They were almost at the trashcan. He felt two arms wrap around his waist and pulled on him as he pulled Sam. Finally, the web stopped with a loud popping noise.

They flew back a couple of feet, and Dylan helped Sam up. "That was way too close," Dylan said. Sam was trying to stand, but he could not put any pressure on his foot. "We need to get you to the nurse." Dylan put Sam's arm around his shoulder. He expected to see JP helping, but he was still catching his breath. Instead, it was Paige on the other side of Sam; she had been the one who had helped pull Sam back from the spiders.

Paige smiled at Dylan. "That was very brave, Dylan."

The butterflies in his stomach were doing flip-flops. She knew his name! Paige, the most beautiful girl in the whole school, knew his name, Dylan thought as he smiled back at her.

"I like your hair." What was he thinking? Surely he could have come up with something better to say.

The bell rang. JP sighed. "I will tell Mrs. Ragoon where you are. You'd better hurry before that spider tries again." He ran off to class.

"Mrs. Ragoon won't like us being late," Dylan said as he started to help Sam to the nurse's office. "They really should get some better bug spray."

Paige laughed as they reached the nurse's office. "You're funny."

They sat Sam down in a chair, and the nurse walked up to them. "What happened?" she asked. Dylan explained about the spiders. The nurse was very nice and she looked young. Her short black hair was pulled down from the right side to cover her left eye. She listened as Dylan spoke.

"So how did he fall? Did he trip?" She was looking into Sam's eyes.

He found his voice. "I was pushed." His voice was shaky. "I am not sure who did it but I felt someone put their . . ." He acted as if he was not sure of what to say next. "Their, well, I guess, their hand." Dylan gave Sam a questioning look but didn't say anything.

"You two should get to class," said the nurse as she examined Sam's ankle. "It looks like a sprain. He should be fine. I will bandage him up and send him back to class. Tell Mrs. Ragoon he will be up in a little while." Her bright red lips smiled as she shooed them out the door.

Dylan was right. His teacher, Mrs. Ragoon, was not happy that they were late. She was an older woman with lots of wrinkles; her white hair stuck out at all angles. The worst part is how she would keep a glass of water on her desk, not to drink, but to put her dentures into when she was done talking. It seemed she was already in a bad mood; a girl named Anna had fallen asleep at her desk. Mrs. Ragoon had a coffin-size box at the back of the room that she called the nap-nap box. Dylan could hear Anna banging on the top.

He took his seat next to JP and tried to focus on the vocabulary words that the teacher was going over. He kept taking quick glances at Paige sitting at her desk across the room. She was smiling at him. Then he started thinking about what Sam had said. "I was pushed." Who would have pushed him? Everyone liked Sam. Dylan kept thinking to himself, "Why would someone want to hurt Sam?"

He had trouble staying out of his own thoughts throughout the morning. He just could not understand why someone had wanted to hurt his friend. Maybe it was a joke, but what a dangerous joke! Everyone knew to stay back from those trashcans. Whoever pushed him knew that they were risking his life. There was so much on his mind and the clock seemed like it had forgotten to move.

Sam still had not come to the room. Maybe I should have stayed with him, Dylan thought as he looked at the clock. The bell finally rang for lunch. The kids got up from their desks and lined up at the door behind Mrs. Ragoon, who had just put her teeth back into her mouth. They headed to the cafeteria. At least now, he would get a closer look at the box.

Dylan went through the lunch line. He grabbed a tray and milk. The lunch ladies all looked the same. They wore what Dylan thought looked like nurse uniforms. The all had smiley faces on them, which made them look depressing because none of them smiled, ever. They scooped different foods on Dylan's tray. "Enjoy your tuna surprise," said the last one as she plopped some grey mushy stuff on his plate. She then took the ladle and scratched her back with it. "Gross," thought Dylan as he headed to get a seat.

Dylan sat at an empty table and looked down at his food. "Is that what they have for lunch today?"

Caleb had come over to him. "Matthew says it's gross, but I am starving, so I am going to try it."

Dylan looked puzzled. "Who is Matthew? Is he your invisible friend?" Dylan rolled his eyes. He hated that his little brother was in his lunch period. Caleb always came to bug him before going to sit at the third grade table with no one around him.

"He's my friend, and he says if you don't stop bullying me, he will sick the wooly ones on you," Caleb said in an angry voice. "I'm going to go get lunch. Goodbye." Caleb walked off to go through the lunch line.

"Everything good?" Terry had come to sit with Dylan. "What was your brother doing?"

Dylan moved his spoon around in his tuna. "He and his imaginary friend Matthew were telling me how gross my lunch looked."

Terry looked at the food and said, "Well, I can't disagree with them. It looks nasty. I wonder what the surprise is in the tuna." Terry had a look of disgust as he looked at the tuna. "So what was going on this morning?"

Dylan told him about the spiders. Terry gave a shiver. "I hate bugs."

JP came and sat next to Dylan. "Well, I got it cleaned up." JP pulled the little box out of his bag. "I washed it the best I could. Some of the paint has chipped off a bit but you can still make out the pictures." He ran his hand over the top of the box. It had a picture of a white crystal that had a green glow around it. "This one looks as if it was on the box since it was made. The rest are carved into the wood." He handed Dylan the box.

Dylan spun the box in his hand. On the front of the box was a carving of what looked like the sun and the moon and in between them looked like a crude drawing of the earth. The next side had a carving of a nest with colored eggs. Dylan turned to look at the back. Here, once again, was a crude carving of what looked like some animal on its hind legs. Also, on the back was a stick figure with a spear. It looked as if it were chasing the animal. Dylan turned the box once more to find a carved circle with three lines crossed through it.

Dylan looked over at the third-grade table. He did not want Caleb to know he had the box. Caleb was having what looked like a heated argument with Matthew. He looked back at JP. "I still have no clue what it all means. I can't even tell what the animal on the back is. Kind of reminds me of a bear."

Terry took the box out of Dylan's hands. "I have seen this box before, but it was not covered in carvings." He looked with interest at the box.

"I could have sworn I have seen this top picture before too," JP said. "I know it had something to do with Hellman, but I can't remember." He took the box from Terry. "As for the carvings, I don't know what that's about."

"Is that the secret box?" Sam asked as he hobbled to Terry's side.

"Thank God, are you okay?" asked Dylan. He got up and gave him a one-armed hug. "I was really worried when you didn't come to class," he said, sitting back down. "What happened?"

"Dad was worried that I had injured my leg so badly that I couldn't play soccer, so he made me go to the emergency room to get x-rays. I'm not quite sure why, but they x-rayed my entire body. It felt very uncomfortable." Sam gave a little shiver. "Turns out it is just a sprained ankle. I have to take it easy for the next few days, but it will heal. Unfortunately, it also means I won't be going to Dino Kingdom tomorrow." He looked a little upset about it.

Dylan couldn't help feeling a twinge of pleasure that Sam was not going to be able to attend the trip. This meant that he could ask Paige to sit with him on the bus. She would probably say no though. Why would the beautiful, popular girl want to sit with him?

Sam smiled as if he could read Dylan's thoughts. "You should totally ask Paige to sit with you on the bus." He pulled up his bandaged foot. "My loss and your gain. I won't be mad at you. I got her to say she would come to my birthday party by telling her you would be there."

Dylan gave Sam a smile that said thanks. "I know you probably don't want to talk about it, but you told the nurse that someone pushed you?"

Sam looked down. "Something pushed me. It felt odd." He ran his fingers through his hair. "I was walking with you guys and then out of nowhere it pushed me. Then I felt the web on my leg and knew I was in trouble. I thought I was a goner." He looked nervous.

"You're not telling us something," JP said, looking at Sam.

Sam looked at them nervously. "It didn't feel like a hand." He looked at the side of the box with the circle that had the three scratches through it. "It seemed like that." He pointed to the lines.

Dylan looked closer at the box, and saw what he had missed. The three lines all merged into what look like a claw. "What do you mean?"

Sam slowly lifted up his shirt to reveal three scratch marks on his back. "It felt like an animal claw." He dropped his shirt back down. "The nurse thinks I got them from when I was struggling against the spider on the floor." He took a deep breath. "Whatever pushed me was not human." The look he was giving was begging his friends to believe him.

"I believe you," said JP. "It's this school. It just keeps getting stranger and stranger."

Dylan didn't always take JP's stories seriously, but he had to admit that something was off. He just wasn't sure what it was yet. He nodded in agreement. "You are one of my best friends. I trust you."

A silence came across them as they thought about what they had learned. Terry broke it a few seconds later. "Look who's walking this way and she has got her eyes on you." He nodded to Dylan.

Dylan quickly put the box into his bag at his feet. Paige was walking toward them. She sat down next to Dylan. "Hey, how's the food?"

Dylan moved the spoon through the soupy tuna once again. "It's pretty disgusting," he said with a laugh.

"I agree, but I would much prefer a bacon double cheeseburger." Paige looked over to Sam. "How is your leg?" she asked, looking at his bandage.

Sam answered, "Just a sprain." Then he looked at Dylan. "Bad news though. I can't go on the field trip. So I guess you will need another bus buddy." Dylan felt him kick his leg with his good foot.

This was his chance; the butterflies were back. Dylan looked at Paige's eyes; they were sparkling green. She smiled at him. Now was the time to be confident. If he didn't do it now, she would get asked by someone else. "Paige, would you want to sit with me?"

Paige never heard Dylan's question. The cafeteria suddenly filled with a high-pitched scream. Dylan looked for the source of the noise. He found it at the third-grade table. Caleb was on his feet, mouth wide open. Dylan stood up. His brother had blood all around his mouth. Dylan watched in horror as Caleb fell back to the table, blood oozing from his lips.

Dylan sat on the bleachers in the gym. Sam, Terry, and JP were sitting with him. "The nurse said that there must have been some glass in the tuna surprise. He tried to swallow it, but the glass cut the roof of his mouth. There was a lot of blood but she got the glass out; she thinks he might have broken a tooth." Dylan was not allowed to stay in the nurse's office with Caleb; he had waited outside her door until she came out and told him that his brother was going to be fine.

"This has been a very bad day," Dylan said. He did not feel it was going to get any better. They were waiting for the PE teacher to come into the gym. Coach Sara was one of the worst teachers at the school. She was a big muscled woman. Her face looked more like a man's; and she had black crinkly hair that came down to her shoulders. She frightened most of the kids at the school and she liked to bully the weaker children.

"Too bad you didn't get a chance to ask Paige to sit with you on the bus." Sam stretched out his legs on the bleacher. "I'm sure she would have said yes."

Coach Sara came out of her office. "Why are you just sitting around on your lazy bums? Get up and start running laps." Everyone started getting up. Coach Sara went over to the bleachers. "Why are you not moving, Samuel?"

Sam looked at her. "I have a hurt foot," he said as he showed her his leg.

"What does that matter? No pain, no gain! Get up and start running!" She pulled him to his feet. "Maybe you could jump on

Terry's back; I hear pterodactyls can fly." She laughed as Sam started to walk as fast as his leg would let him.

After they did twenty laps, Coach Sara made them do jumping jacks, toe touches, sit-ups and push-ups. Dylan stayed close to Sam who looked like he was in a lot of pain. "You okay, bro?" he asked.

Sam had sweat pouring down his face. "It really hurts, but I refuse to quit. That's what she wants." He shifted his weight onto his better leg. Dylan looked over to see Coach Sara giving Terry a hard time about wearing glasses.

After a few more exercises, they were told to hit the showers. After he was done in the locker room, Dylan grabbed his bag from the corner of the gym. He waited for his friends. JP was normally the first one out.

"So that was a fun class," JP said sarcastically. "My legs are sore, and I can't believe she made Sam do all the exercises." Sam was walking toward them with Terry. They grabbed their bags. "Well I guess it's time to head back to class," JP said. He turned to walk away and slammed straight into Coach Sara.

"Watch where I'm walking," she glared down at JP. "Dylan, before you go to class, Principal Schmitt would like to see you in her office."

"I didn't do anything wrong," Dylan said before he could stop himself.

Coach Sara gave a dark laugh. "Sounds like you have a guilty conscience."

Dylan looked at the others. Most people did not like going to the principal's office. The ones who came back usually did not like to talk about what had happened in there. Hoisting his bag onto his shoulder, he left his three friends and headed to certain death.

He got to the principal's office and knocked on the door. There was no answer. Maybe he should just go back to class. He knocked again. The door opened. Taking a deep breath, he entered the room. No one was there. Looking around, he saw pictures of past principals and behind her desk was a very large portrait of herself. He saw an ugly-looking chair; it looked like a skinned grizzly bear. He figured he might as well sit and wait until Principal Schmitt came back.

He looked at the grizzly head that sat on top of the chair. It looked so real. He was just about to sit down when the principal entered the room. "Good afternoon."

Dylan jumped. The arm of the chair caught his bag and ripped it open. The small wooden box fell out and hit the floor. Dylan reached for it, but the principal was faster. She picked it up and held it tight in her pencil-like fingers. "Where did you get this?" she asked.

"It's my mom's. May I please have it back?" Dylan had never seen the principal smile like the way she was as she looked at the box. It was creepy, he thought. She did not answer him but continued to stare at the box. "Please, may I have it back?" He didn't want to sound demanding or rude, but he also didn't like that she had taken it without his consent, which he would not have given her anyway.

She ran her fingers over the carvings. Looking up, she still had the creepy smile. "Sorry, you may have it back." She handed it to him, and then she went and looked at her calendar. "Time sure does fly," she said aloud to the room. "Please have a seat." She pointed to the grizzly chair.

Dylan sat down. He stuffed the box back into his bag, in the portion not ripped. "You wanted to see me?" He was starting to get nervous. Had she found out that he had copied JP's math homework? Then an even worse thought occurred to him. What if she thought he had something to do with Sam and Caleb getting hurt? He was there for both accidents.

She sat down behind her desk. "Now I know that you have had a hard day. First, your best friend gets hurt, then your little brother. Not a fun day." She opened one of her desk drawers.

Dylan looked in horror as she pulled out a human head and sat it on the desk. He backed further into the chair and thought he heard a growl. She turned the head toward him. "Do you like my Halloween present?"

Dylan took a closer look at the head. He realized that it had buttons. The mouth which Dylan thought was open in a horrified scream looked like a speaker. He relaxed a little.

"Your grandmother asked that I have you call her." She pulled one of the ears off the head and handed it to Dylan. It still had a cord running to the head. She looked into the mouth and said "Call Mrs. Rook." The eyes started to glow. Dylan put the ear up to his and heard a ringing. The head was a telephone.

"Hello," came his grandmother's voice.

Feeling some relief he said, "Grandma, it's me, Dylan. Principal Schmitt said you wanted to talk to me."

"Yes, honey, I am stuck at work until seven tonight. I heard about Caleb's accident and I have made him an appointment with Dr. Rajh right after school. He wants to look at that broken tooth. I hate to ask, but will you please take him to the appointment?"

His grandmother was silent waiting for the answer. "Caleb never behaves at the dentist," Dylan said. "I guess, but do I still have to clean my room?"

His grandmother laughed. "Not today, I guess. I will see you when I get home."

Dylan heard the click as she hung up. He handed the principal back the ear. She was not smiling as she put the phone back in the drawer. "Go to class," she said quietly. She didn't have to tell him twice. He jumped up and left the office.

The rest of the day went about normally. Mrs. Ragoon had given the usual homework. When the bell finally rang to end school for the day, Dylan was ready to go home. He was starting to unlock his bike when his brother came out. His mouth looked swollen. "I don't wanna go." He had tears in his eyes.

Dylan felt sorry for him. "Grandma says you have to go. It won't be that bad."

Tears were streaming down Caleb's face, and Dylan could barely understand him. "He knew. He tried to make me not eat. I should have listened to Matthew."

"Great," Dylan thought, "he's going to blame his imaginary friend." Then Caleb said something that made his heart stop. It may have been hard to understand, but he knew what his brother was saying. "Matthew also says that your box is cursed."

VI

Dylan sat in a hardback chair in the dentist office's waiting room. Caleb was holding his hand. It had taken almost a half hour to get him in the door. Caleb had never liked going to the dentist; he was scared of the noise. Dylan didn't care too much about the dentist either. His teeth were in mostly good shape, but the smell of fluoride was obnoxious.

The front door opened and Terry walked in. He went up to the desk and signed his name on the clipboard. He turned and saw Dylan. "Hey, you all right?" he said, looking at Caleb.

Caleb squeezed Dylan's hand tighter but said nothing. "He's a little nervous," Dylan answered.

Terry sat down next to him. "I understand that. I don't like having my teeth touched." He picked up a magazine and flipped through it.

Caleb was looking at him with a frightened look. "Matthew says that the box is going to go after you next."

Terry gave a puzzled look as Dylan responded. "His imaginary friend told him my box is cursed." Dylan pulled the box out of his bag. "I still can't get it to open, so I'm just going to put it back where I found it."

Caleb looked at the box. "It's too late; he already knows."

Dylan was getting more and more worried about his brother. He was not making any sense. The tuna accident must have really gotten to him. The little box could not be cursed, could it? He thought. Sam had an accident right after they had been talking about it. Then Caleb got hurt when he had the box out at lunch. Was there a connection?

The dentist walked out wearing a suit and tie. Dylan thought he looked out of place. "Good afternoon," the dentist spoke with a British accent. When he smiled, he showed off his crooked, yellow teeth. It definitely did not invite confidence. "Mr. Dactyl, Mr. Rook, we need to do some x-rays. We are going to get a look at the inside of your smile." He laughed at his pun. "I promise it will only take a few minutes."

Terry stood up, but Caleb gave Dylan a look that plainly said, "Don't leave me."

"Don't worry," Terry took Caleb's other hand, "we can do it together." Caleb took a deep breath and stood up. They went with the dentist into the back room.

As the door shut, the front one opened, and Dylan caught a smell of fresh strawberries. He turned in his seat to see Paige walk in. He stood up. "I like your teeth."

She looked at him. "Thanks," she replied slowly as she went to sign in. "I like my teeth too." She smiled and sat down.

Just like the last time he had spoken to her, his mouth just vomited the first thing that came to his mind. He felt himself going red. How embarrassing! Why could he not have said something cool like Sam would have said? He felt as if he should crawl into the corner and act dead. But he figured he would give it one more shot. "So what are you doing here?" Right away, he wished he had crawled into the corner.

Paige looked at him and smiled. "Well, most people come to the dentist to have their teeth checked. I, however, am here to have my eyes examined." She laughed. "You don't have to be nervous around me; I won't bite you." She moved a strand of hair out of her eyes by shaking her head to the left.

Dylan took a breath. "Sorry, it's just that, well . . ." He was not sure what to say, but this was the first time they had ever been alone together. "I have a crush on you." He said the last part fast like tearing off a Band-Aid. He expected her to act surprised or to even move away from him.

Paige laughed. "Well, that was kind of obvious." She moved closer. "Is your brother all right? That was a lot of blood."

Dylan gulped. "Yeah, the nurse said it looked like a broken tooth. His mouth is swollen. That's why Grandma sent him here." Now that the conversation was going, Dylan did not want it to stop. "He's not a big fan of the dentist. He's on the spectrum."

"Wow, it's so nice of you to take care of him like you do," Paige said. "My older brother acts like I am his slave. It's 'Paige get me a drink, clean my room.' Such a jerk." She rolled her eyes.

Dylan was starting to feel the butterflies leave his stomach. Now would be the perfect time to ask her. He opened his mouth, but right then, both Caleb and Terry came back out. Caleb grabbed Dylan. "That was awful. They made me open my mouth too wide and now it hurts even worse. It's bad. I think they want to cut out my teeth."

Dylan looked from Paige to Caleb. "Now why do you think that?" He was trying to get him to calm down. "Did Matthew tell you that? If so, I am sure he is wrong."

This did nothing to help calm Caleb. "It was not him that said it. It was the nurse." Caleb started to fidget with his shirt. He sat down next to Dylan but looked very anxious.

Terry looked at Dylan. "I tried my best to keep him calm. He liked looking at all the fish in the tank back there." Terry nodded to Paige. He leaned in to Dylan's right side and whispered, "The nurses did seem a little freaked out with the x-ray, but I don't know why."

Dylan understood that Terry was trying to make sure that Caleb was not able to overhear. Dylan looked at him as he shrugged. All they could do now was wait until the dentist called them back. The dentist came back out. "Ms. Hilton, right this way please." Paige got up and left the room.

Terry looked at Dylan with a wide smile. "So did you ask her?"

Looking frustrated, Dylan replied, "I was about to when you two came back out." At this rate, he felt that he would never get around to asking Paige to sit with him tomorrow. Maybe she would not have anyone to sit with, so he would just sit with her on the bus tomorrow.

"I hear that some fifth grader is going to call and ask her to hang out with him," Terry said. A nurse came out of the office door. "All right, you two, time to get cleaned up."

Caleb looked at Dylan with a sad face and said, "Please come with me."

Dylan nodded. "Let me grab my bag, and I will be right behind you." Caleb and Terry walked out. Dylan bent over to get his bag from behind the chair, when he overheard two nurses talking.

"Did you see that boy's x-ray?" the first one asked.

"Oh my, yes. That cannot be normal, and it was not just one or two teeth but all of them," came the reply from the second.

"I had better take Dr. Rajh the results. I just feel so sorry for that poor boy. He is going to go through a lot of pain," the first nurse said as she walked out.

Dylan went through the door and found Caleb in a chair with a bright light over his head. The nurse had given him a pair of safety glasses to put on. Dylan watched as Caleb squirmed around as the nurse cleaned his teeth. "Almost done, just got to pull that back tooth." Caleb jerked so hard that his arm hit a folder on the counter, knocking it to the floor.

Dylan bent down to pick it up when a black slide fell out. He picked it up; it could not be right. He looked at the name on the back: C. Rook. He held it up to the light blocking it out of his brother's view. Dylan could not believe his eyes; something had gone wrong with the x-rays. Looking closer, he saw rows of teeth that looked like they were under the gum, but they looked odd. They looked as if they belonged in the mouth of a shark, not a human!

Dylan straightened up. As he put the file back onto the counter, he slipped the x-ray into his pocket. Dr. Rajh entered the room. "All right, Mr. Rook, let's get that bad boy out of your mouth." He pulled out a pair of dentist pliers. He put his fingers into Caleb's mouth. "I think we might need some help holding you down. I will be right back." He left.

Dylan looked at the large aquarium dividing Caleb's chair from the next patient. He could see Terry having his teeth cleaned through the glass. He saw a fish swim by. "What kind of fish are those?" he asked to the room in general.

"Piranhas," said Dr. Rajh as he walked back in with two nurses. "I love them, but you don't want to go sticking your hand in there." He laughed. "All right, let's do this." The two nurses held Caleb's legs and arms.

Paige walked by the door, and looked in at Dylan. Now was his last chance; he had to do it. "Paige, would you like to sit with me on the bus?" The words came out in a rush.

Paige blinked. "Sure, sounds fun. See you in the morning." She walked on and Dylan returned to watching Caleb. His spirits were soaring. He had done it, and he had not messed it up. Best of all, she said yes. This day had gone from bad to good. He was going to be riding the bus with the hottest girl in the class. Nothing could have taken away his feeling of jubilation. Nothing except what happened next.

It all went so fast. Caleb was struggling against the nurses as the dentist was trying to pull the tooth out. The dentist got it. He raised the broken tooth up with the pliers just as Caleb got his arm free. Dylan watched as Caleb's hand knocked the pliers out of the dentist's grip. They soared in the air and crashed straight through the glass aquarium. Glass and water went everywhere. Caleb had gotten out of the chair. Dylan grabbed him by the arm. The doctor and nurses were wiping their faces; they were fine. At first, it didn't register that someone was screaming, but then Dylan looked over and saw two piranhas sinking their teeth into Terry's stomach!

Dylan jumped over the divide that was between him and Terry. He grabbed a silver tray with the instruments that were on it, and it clanged to the floor. He swung the tray at the fish and knocked them off Terry's body. Terry was frozen in shock; he tried to get up but couldn't. The dentist came in, but instead of worrying about Terry, he scooped up the fish and put them into some water.

Caleb was standing next to Dylan. "Matthew was right again."

Dylan could not take his eyes off Terry. Dylan thought to himself, "Was Terry the third victim of the mysterious box? Could it just be a coincidence?" He walked over to Terry. The fish had bitten him hard, but the bites did not seem to be deep. He helped him out of the chair. His legs were wobbly, but he was able to stand.

"I think I'm okay," he said. "I just think I need to go home."

The dentist was still dealing with his fish. Dylan nodded. "Yeah, let's get out of here." As they walked to the door, Dylan saw Terry's file. His x-ray was paper clipped to the top; his teeth looked normal. If Terry's teeth were normal, then there must not have been anything wrong with the x-ray machine.

The three boys rode their bikes home. By the time they got there, it was nearly seven o'clock. Terry said that he was feeling better and headed into his house. Dylan and Caleb took their bikes around to the back of the house. Dylan stopped in surprise. There was a huge hole dug in the ground. Bonedigger rushed forward out of the hole, dragging a bone that was the size of a gorilla's arm.

He placed the bone at Dylan's feet, obviously hoping to get a "Good job, boy" and a pat on the head. Neither of the boys moved. Bonedigger gave a bark while wagging his tail. Caleb looked at the bone closer. "We need to cover this up before Grandma gets home."

They grabbed an old bedsheet, wrapped the bone up, then hid it in the garage. They got shovels and filled in the hole just as their grandma came into the driveway.

The boys went inside to get ready for dinner. They ate in silence, both thinking about the day's events and the large bone in their garage. "Why are you two so silent?" asked their grandma.

Looking at each other, they both replied, "Just tired. Excited for the trip in the morning."

"Well then, I guess you two had better go on to bed," she said.

They got up and left the table. Caleb went into his room as Dylan shut the door to his bedroom. He got into his pajamas and lay down in his bed. His mind was racing. So many people had gotten hurt today. Was it really because of the box? If it were cursed, then who would the next victim be? He rolled onto his side. What if he were next? What if it were Paige? Each incident could have been fatal. Would the next person be as lucky?

He wasn't sure when his thoughts and dreams combined, but he was running in slow motion. Looking back, he saw Caleb, but it was not his brother anymore. He had become a monster. A monster with razor-sharp teeth. Caleb had Paige in his hands.

"I should have sat with Sam. He would have known how to work the box. It's your fault I got cursed," Paige screamed as Caleb ate her whole. Suddenly, Dylan tripped over a large bone. He fell on his back. Caleb stuck out his tongue and licked Dylan's face.

He woke with a start. Bonedigger had been lying next to him, licking his face. Not Caleb, Bonedigger the dog. He pushed the dog off him, turned over, and fell back to sleep.

VII

The next morning Dylan awoke a little sore but excited. He had totally forgotten about the dream he had during the night. He had set his alarm for an hour earlier than usual, as he wanted to take a shower before riding the bus with Paige. He went to his closet. "What should I wear?" Pushing some shirts aside, he looked for a shirt that would say, "Hey, I'm a cool guy!" Finally, he decided on his "Real Men Wear Pink" shirt.

He grabbed a pair of skinny jeans from his dresser and headed to the bathroom. He took his time in the shower, went over his entire body twice, and washed his hair three times. He wrapped a towel around his waist, looked into the mirror, and started messing with his hair. He tried a few different styles trying to make himself look cooler, but in the end, he decided it would be better to be himself. He grabbed the stick of deodorant and rubbed it on his back, chest and under his arms.

Deciding that he looked good, he opened the bathroom door to find Caleb standing there. "I thought you were drowning in there." Caleb sniffed the air and pretended to choke. "Are you trying to hide dead fish or something?

Dylan realized that his brother had returned to being his obnoxious self again. "Well, I am glad you came to save me. Just let me jump onto those ears." He moved past him. Caleb grabbed his arm and sank his teeth into his skin.

Dylan jerked his arm out of Caleb's mouth. "What are you doing? Have you completely lost your mind?" Looking down, he saw the teeth marks on his skin.

"Quit making fun of my ears or the wooly will get you!" Caleb entered the bathroom and shut the door.

Dylan made his way into the kitchen and fixed a bowl of cereal. He opened his backpack and took out the wooden box. He had been thinking about it while he was in the shower. He was going to put it back where he found it. That way no one else would get hurt. As he stood up, his grandma walked into the kitchen. Not wanting to be in trouble for taking his mom's things, he shoved the box back into his backpack.

She was brushing dirt off her jeans. "We are going to have to do something about that dog."

Puzzled, Dylan asked, "Why? What did he do?"

His grandmother opened the window blinds to show the backyard. "Holes, a dozen of them. I haven't seen this many since your mom was twelve years old. That's when she wanted to be an archeologist. Every day she would come home and dig in the backyard, looking for dinosaur bones." She rolled her eyes. "It will take me forever to fill all these holes. Maybe I should plant some flowers."

Dylan looked out the window. The backyard was covered in holes. He turned as Caleb and Bonedigger entered the kitchen. Bonedigger ran to Dylan and jumped up on him to lick his face. Pushing him off, Dylan said, "Check out what Bonedigger did last night."

Caleb looked out the window. "That's a lot of holes, but Bonedigger could not have done that since he was in my room all night long." He gave Dylan a meaningful look. "We should get to school. Come on, Dylan, we don't want to miss the field trip." He grabbed Dylan's arm and dragged him outside.

Expecting to go to their bikes, Dylan was surprised when they passed them. "Where are we going?"

"The bone, the one Bonedigger had last night. I want to make sure it's safe," Caleb answered.

"I'm sure it is fine. The garage was locked." However, as they got closer, Dylan saw that the door was slightly open. He pushed it all the way and looked at the lock; it had been torn apart. It had three claw marks running across it. Caleb ran to where they had hid the bone. He pulled out the tangled bedsheet. The bone was gone.

"Who would want a dirty old bone?" Caleb asked.

"I don't know. But whoever took it must have thought there were more. That's why they dug more holes," Dylan said as he continued to look at the broken door. "We had better get to school." They grabbed their bikes and headed out.

They reached the school to find Terry locking up his bike. "Hey, the upper grades are meeting in the gym before the field trip." They locked up their bikes and walked into the school.

Dylan was in a hurry as he wanted to talk to JP. He saw him sitting with Sam and went over to them. "How's your ankle?" He didn't give Sam a chance to respond. "I think the box might be cursed. I think it's my fault everyone got hurt yesterday."

Terry sat down. "It's not your fault. You didn't put glass in your brother's tuna and you didn't throw those stupid fish at me."

Sam chimed in. "You definitely did not push me. You were next to me. I tried to grab your arm before I went down. If that box is cursed, we need to destroy it."

JP nodded and said, "But we should do more research first."

Dylan took a deep breath. "There's more. I think there is something wrong with Caleb."

Sam laughed. "So what's new?"

Dylan pulled out the x-ray slide. "Look at this. His teeth look like an animal's. Also, last night somebody broke into our garage and stole a bone that Bonedigger found. The only other person that knew about the bone was Caleb."

JP took the slide out of Dylan's hands and held it up. Both Terry and Sam leaned closer to see it. "Are these his teeth?" Each of them sat quietly looking at the slide.

"I found them in his file at the dentist's office." Dylan said.

"Quiet!" came his principal's voice.

The gym became silent as the principal continued. "I hope you are all ready for our wonderful field trip." Her face was stone-cold. "The buses will be leaving in five minutes. If you are not going on the trip, you will stay seated. Dr. Bates will be taking you to the cafeteria to take a test to see how much you have learned this year."

"But we have only been in school for a few weeks," came the voice of a third grader whose name Dylan did not know. The principal looked at him with her dark eyes. "I expect everyone to make a C or higher." The boy drew closer to his friends in fear.

The principal returned her attention to the group. "We will be taking bus 13 and bus 31. Go get seated." She walked out of the gym.

Dylan got up. "I'm riding with Paige. I had better find her."

Sam looked sad, but he sighed and said, "Have fun, I'll let you know how the test goes."

Dylan walked outside and found Paige by bus 13. They climbed the steps and found a seat near the back of the bus. She put her hand in his and smiled. He could feel his face growing hot. JP and Terry were sitting in the seats in front of them. He could see them looking over the seat.

"This is going to be so much fun. I love dinosaurs," Paige said.

Dylan, a little shyly, said, "Me too. My mommy digs them up." He felt childish. "Their bones, I mean. She is an archaeologist. She is always off on an adventure, digging up stuff." He seemed to have caught her interest. "Oh, she has uncovered lots of things—bones, mummies, caves. She is very busy." As he said it, a sad feeling washed over him.

JP turned in his seat. "You know this field trip could end up being like the movie where the group of people go on a tour and get eaten by the dinosaurs."

Terry gave him a look that plainly said "Shut up."

"You mean *Jurassic Park*? The dinosaurs at Dino Kingdom are made of wax. I don't think they will eat you. This won't be a Jurassic field trip."

Paige shook her hair. "You are so strange, JP." She gave a little laugh as she looked at Dylan. "That's so cool that your mom gets to travel all over the world. I feel like I will be stuck here in Golfing Blue forever. Do you ever take trips with her?"

"No, she never lets me or my brother come." Dylan wanted to change the subject. He didn't want to think about his mom. Now he was feeling angry with her. He thought about the little box in his bag and that maybe he should just toss it out the window of the bus.

The buses were filled and a large round man climbed onto the bus. It was Marty, the school's grossest bus driver. Dylan was very glad they had chosen seats at the back of the bus. However, even in the back, he could smell Marty's feet. Marty was dressed in his usual bus uniform of blue slacks, which he didn't bother pulling up before he sat down, and a white T-shirt that Dylan did not think had been washed in weeks due to the yellow armpit stains. He wore sandals because his long yellowed toenails couldn't fit into shoes.

He pulled the doors closed; there was apprehension on the faces of the few teachers who were sitting up front, including Mrs. Ragoon. Putting his finger into his belly button to pull out the lent, he began speaking. "Welcome to bus 13, or as I like to call it, my home. That being said, please treat my home with respect, and if you are in the back, please do not eat my food." Looking down, Dylan saw Ziploc baggies of moldy sandwiches.

Marty continued. "Also, should the need arise and you have to pee, just swing open the back door and go; it doesn't lock." He took his seat and started to adjust the mirrors. "Now I have been informed that it should take around thirty minutes to reach our destination. However, last year I made it in eighteen minutes and thirteen seconds. I hope to break my record this year, so please do not stand up while the bus is in motion. If ya gotta barf, please wait until we arrive and use the barf bags at the front of the bus. I don't like the smell."

He hit the gas; they went from zero to fifty in three seconds. Dylan grabbed hold of the chair in front of him. He felt Paige put her head on his shoulder. Terry had a look on his face as the bus took a curve, and he covered his mouth. JP, who normally rode the bus to school, didn't seemed fazed by Marty's driving skills. The bus didn't stop for anything. It blew through red lights and stop signs. It swerved in and out of traffic, sometimes hitting the curb.

Dylan tried to talk to Paige, but she shook her head and shut her eyes. The bus took a sharp turn, sending Paige and Dylan slamming into the window. He looked out and saw the world flying by and felt his stomach churning. The bus turned and Dylan caught himself by grabbing the chair before he fell out of his seat.

Over the sound of groaning and retching, he heard Marty's voice, "Five miles to go—gonna set a new record."

Dylan was gripping his hands to the chair in front of him. The bus jumped the curb and came to a screeching halt in the gravel parking lot of Dino Kingdom. Everybody lurched forward into the seat in front of them. Marty jumped to his feet opening the door. "All right, everyone out. Hope you enjoyed the ride."

Students made a mad dash for the exit grabbing the barf bags as they exited. Mrs. Ragoon was searching the bus floor for her teeth. Terry, Paige, and Dylan dizzily walked past her; JP walked out normally. "After a while, you get used to it," he said and began walking to the entrance of the park.

Looking around, Dylan saw that there was a large Brontosaur standing over the parking lot. He looked at the stone building ahead. There were duckbilled dinosaurs on each side of the glass doors. Still feeling slightly sick, he walked forward. The words "Welcome to Dino Kingdom" were in large red letters on top of what reminded him of Stonehenge.

Terry stumbled forward. "It looks like something out of the Stone Age." He stood up straight and Dylan saw a look of terror. He pointed to something over Dylan's shoulder. "Dylan, move!"

"It's okay, man, we are off the bus." Dylan turned to see what Terry was pointing at and his mouth dropped open in shock. It was coming over the building; gigantic, green, and angry. Dylan's legs gave out and he fell to the ground as the T-Rex's mouth opened in a deafening roar. It lowered its head, looking straight at Dylan. He could see the sharp row of teeth as the T-Rex came at him.

VIII

Dylan braced for the jaws to clamp shut around him. He could feel its hot breath. Then he felt a soft hand tugging on his arm. Paige was pulling him up saying, "It's not real, just a robot."

He took a deep breath and looked up at the roaring T-Rex. Now that he was looking at it closer, he could see that it was not a living dinosaur. The head and arms were jerking in an awkward motion, and its skin looked too loose. He could hear other students laughing at him. He could not believe that he fell in front of Paige.

"Don't be embarrassed. The first time I saw him I freaked out too." Paige gave him an encouraging smile. "In all honesty, they picked the biggest wimp to put at the front gates. Everyone thinks that the T-Rex was all big and bad, but he couldn't hurt a fly, scared of his own tail. They should have put Spinney up there. Now that guy was terrifying." She looked up in disgust at the poorly done robot.

There was the sound of a door closing. "Everything all right out here?" A security guard had walked out of his little station. He was a big man and wore a blue shirt with the words "DINO SECURITY" printed on the back. His tan trousers looked like clown pants and were held up by purple suspenders. His hat was pulled down over his ears. He pushed his dark sunglasses up his nose, which looked as if it had been broken and had healed wrong, causing it to point upward.

The first thought that went through Dylan's mind was, "Why does a museum of wax dinosaurs need security guards?" The guard gave him a look that made him feel as if he were being x-rayed. The rest of the students were looking at the guard in silence.

The guard removed his sunglasses, revealing dark-green eyes. "You must be the kids for the field trip. We weren't expecting you to arrive so quickly. I will go let Alex know you are here. He's gonna be your tour guide." He laughed and walked back into his guard shack.

Dylan watched the guard walk back to the guard shack; he had a strange walk. Dylan turned his attention back to Paige. "So how many times have you been here?" He was glad that everyone had started talking in little groups. The only two that were listening to him were JP and Terry.

Paige pulled a card out of her bag and showed it to him. "My family has a season pass. I come every few weeks." She put the card back. "I told you I was obsessed with dinosaurs." They talked about fifteen minutes while they waited for the second bus to arrive.

When it finally pulled in under the giant *Brontosaurus*, Dylan watched the bus come to a stop. It obviously had been a much smoother ride than his had been. As students started walking off, he saw Caleb slowly walk down the steps to the gravel parking lot. It seemed as if he were nervous. He had been so excited about this trip. Dylan wondered what had caused him to change his attitude.

The next person who came off the bus made his heart drop. Coach Sara was lumbering down the steps. She looked a little bit off; her muscles seemed larger than usual and her hair was wild. She glanced in his direction and gave him an evil grin.

The teachers started herding the students to the front doors. Dylan saw a young man walk out; his immediate thought was "What a geek." The man, who looked to be in his early twenties, had flaming red hair and a face full of freckles. He was dressed in khakis and a button down white-collar shirt tucked into his pants. His glasses had tape around the bridge, keeping them together, so he had to continually push them up his nose as he spoke.

"Welcome to the kingdom of the dinosaurs. My name is Alex and I will be guiding you through our dangerous jungles." His voice had a whiny feel to it. "This is a place where dreams come true. You will see things that have been extinct for millions of years. Our park is forty-eight acres of walking trails. But be careful—you never know when a dino will get hungry for a snack."

He laughed and pointed to the robot T-Rex, which was roaring once more. "No need to fear as long as you stay on the walking paths. We have over one hundred wax dinosaurs for you to enjoy. Also, for your enjoyment, we have the boneyard—you can dig for your own fossils, and you might even find some spectacular surprises."

Alex looked as if he enjoyed his job just a little too much. "Please remember these simple rules. One, don't touch the exhibits. Two, no going past the yellow tape. And three, no food allowed in the park as our dinos are on a strict diet. And finally, have fun learning!" Alex clapped his hands and the doors opened.

Dylan walked in the double doors. He wasn't sure what to expect as he entered a room full of toys and stuffed dinosaurs. It was the gift shop. Alex began again. "Your tour begins and ends right here in our wonderful gift shop. I will be out on the paths to answer any questions you might have. As you exit the gift shop, your journey through the Jurassic begins."

Slowly, kids started moving to the door labeled "To the Dinosaurs." Caleb banged into Dylan's back, smiling as he went out the door. Dylan held back; he wanted to be behind everyone with Paige.

There was a tap on his arm. It was Terry. "Look." He pointed to shelves at the back of the gift shop. There, sitting on the shelves, were little wooden boxes. They walked closer, and Terry picked up one of the boxes. He turned to show the top to Dylan. He knew what he was going to see before Terry had picked it up. The top had the same painting of a crystal that his mom's box had.

Terry handed the box to Dylan while JP, looking interested, and Paige, looking puzzled, watched. He turned the box in his hand; there were no other carvings or pictures. He looked at the shelf and read the item description. "Puzzle Box. $22.95. Keep your secret guarded with your very own puzzle security system. Each box has a different puzzle. No one but you will break the code."

"You can buy gifts at the end of the day! Get a move on!" Coach Sara had snuck up on them.

Putting up the box, they turned and headed to the walking paths. As they exited the door, Dylan noticed the guard watching him. It made him uncomfortable, like he was in trouble. Did the guard know what he had in his bag? Why was a puzzle box from Dino Kingdom in his mom's room? He pushed the thoughts out as he took Paige's hand. He wanted to focus on having a good time. They started out on their journey through the jungle with a smile.

Dylan walked slowly with Paige through the hot man-made jungle. He was finding it easier to talk to her. JP and Terry had walked on ahead. The dirt path was filled with small holes, so they were careful not to trip. Every so often they would stop and look at the exhibits. They stopped in front of a *Velociraptor* section. Dylan looked into the eyes of the wax dinosaurs. There were three of them; the design of the exhibit made it look as if they were preparing an attack.

Dylan leaned on the wooden three-split fence. The two dinosaurs to the left and right looked almost identical. Their black eyes looked as if they were carelessly glued onto the side of the head. Their long tails were held rigid behind them as they stood on two legs. They had two little arms ending with a three-nailed claw. The green skin had a waxy glow in the sunlight.

Dylan looked into the green eyes of the center dinosaur. This one looked more realistic; the tail didn't seem as stiff. It was also missing the waxy shine, but that may have been because it was more in the shadows of the trees. It was so lifelike that Dylan even thought he could see the belly move up and down as it breathed.

"They look so fake, don't they?" asked Paige. "The guy in the center looks good. More accurate anyway."

Dylan leaned closer to the small plaque explaining the exhibit. "These are Velociraptors; they are thought to be one of the deadlier dinos in the kingdom, with three four-inch claws on each foot."

Paige stopped him from reading anymore. "Just because some scientist said so doesn't make it true. These guys were just big teddy bears. The meat ripping claws were for tearing bark off trees. Just like the rex, they are misunderstood. Those claws were also good back scratchers."

Dylan shielded his eye from the sun and replied, "Where did you learn all this?"

"Mainly from my older brother; he is a dinosaur nutjob," Paige said as she tugged him away from the velociraptors. He gave them one last glance and started walking. He was not sure why, but he had a feeling that he was being watched as they moved to the next exhibit.

They continued walking and talking about school and their families. As they went by different dinosaurs, they would stop and Paige would talk about how they had gotten things wrong. They passed all sorts of prehistoric animals; some looked more realistic than others.

They came to another dinosaur, *Dilophosaurus*. Standing on the bottom rung of the fence was Caleb. Not really wanting to spoil his fun with Paige, he was going to skip this one. She chimed, "The *Dilophosaurus!* They are my all-time favorite!"

Caleb turned around and gave Dylan a mischievous grin. "What you doing, bro?"

"Just walking," Dylan replied. He looked at the lone wax dinosaur. It was just a little bit taller than he was; the snout was long and showed sharp teeth. It had a crest around its neck that reminded Dylan of a lizard that walked on water. It had a strong-looking tail with small spikes going up its spine. Most of the other dinosaurs that they had passed had been a greenish color, but this one's skin was a light blue.

"Isn't it beautiful?" Paige had a strange look in her eyes.

Caleb chose that moment to become his bratty self. "Is this your girlfriend? Are you going to kiss her?" He took Paige's hand. "You don't want to kiss him. It's gross. I saw him kiss Grandma once and it was nasty. There was spit all over. If you do kiss him, you better have a towel ready."

Dylan punched him hard in the arm. "Do you have to be so annoying?"

"I'm the little brother; it's my job." Caleb jumped up and down. "Have fun k-i-s-s-i-n-g." He spelled out the word *kissing*. He ran back down the path. Dylan looked at where Caleb had been standing. He ran his hand over three stark marks left in the wood where Caleb's hand had been.

Paige's laugh brought him out of his thoughts. "My brother was interested in the *Dilophosaurus*. He believed that the head crest was very important; it was their protection."

Dylan looked at the wax figure once more, "Those are some big claws. I would not want to tick him off." He was trying to get her to laugh again. He liked seeing her smile. She didn't smile; a gloomy look came over her smooth face. Did he say something wrong, he thought to himself with nervous worry.

Paige took Dylan's hand. She had a look of worry in her green eyes. "Can I trust you? Can you keep a secret?"

Dylan saw a look of urgency in her eyes. "Anything you tell me will stay between us."

Paige took a deep breath. "It's about my brother. He would be so mad if I told you what happened. He always told me to trust no one. But I don't know what to do anymore."

Dylan stood frozen; he did not expect this. He saw tears forming in her eyes. "I promise I won't tell anyone." Even as he said it, he felt his mouth going dry.

"My brother, Allen, disappeared," Paige stuttered. Before she could get the next word out, they were once again interrupted, this time by Alex.

Alex was walking down the path with a group of kids, including Caleb. "Hurry back to the raptor pen. Lunch is ready to be served. I am sure all your walking has built up your appetite."

Dylan saw Caleb snicker and mouthed the word "walking." As he walked by Dylan, he could hear Caleb saying, "Kissing maybe."

Alex paid no attention. "I do hope you are enjoying our two wonderful wax models of the Dilophosaurus. After lunch we will—"

Caleb interrupted him. "Two? There's only one. Maybe you need to clean your glasses."

Alex took a double look at the exhibit. "Well, I thought there were two. Maybe it's just behind the trees. Anyway, after lunch, I will be showing you our most prized dinosaur, *Spinosaurus*. It's a marvel. Now hurry along."

The group moved back down the path. Dylan pulled Paige to the back and whispered, "Sorry about that. Maybe we can find a more private place to talk after lunch." She smiled and gave his hand a squeeze.

They walked in silence behind everyone else. Once they reached the picnic tables across from the raptors, they sat down at the one table that was farthest from everyone else. Just as Dylan was about to ask her about her brother, his eyes fell on the raptors. The two waxy figures looked just as they did earlier. The problem was that they were the only two there; the middle one was gone.

Dylan stared at the exhibit; there had been three. He wasn't losing his mind. Where had it gone? It could not have just run off, could it? Dylan looked around; nobody else seemed to care that there was a missing dinosaur.

Paige noticed the look of concern on Dylan's face. "What's wrong? You look like you have seen a ghost."

"I swear there were three raptors, but now there are only two. I think that I am losing my mind," Dylan replied in a strained voice.

Unfortunately, he was overhead by Coach Sara. She slammed her beefy hands down on the picnic table, making both Dylan and Paige jump. "You can't lose what you don't got," she heckled. Dylan could smell her breath as she spoke. "So you think that a rouge dinosaur is on the rampage?" She wasn't bothering to keep her voice down. Dylan would not have been surprised if Sam could hear her all the way back at the school. "Well, if you see any more dinos on the loose, please let us know. Of course, your brother might be the most dangerous thing in this place." She walked on to pick on some fifth grader that Dylan didn't know.

Dylan looked over at his brother; he was tearing off a strip of meat from his turkey leg. There is something really wrong with him, Dylan thought. He looked at Paige. "Well, this has been a really nice time."

Paige lowered her voice. "There were three, and there were two *Dilophosaurus*. It's this place. I have seen things. Things that if you tell people, they would think that you were crazy."

Dylan took a second look at Caleb; he was now gnawing on the bone of the turkey leg. "Like people turning into monsters?"

Paige looked puzzled. "What do you mean?"

"It's Caleb. He has been acting weird ever since the accident yesterday. At the dentist, I . . . I saw his x-ray. His teeth aren't normal." They were both now staring at Caleb. "Then our garage was broken into and the lock looked as if it had been torn apart by claws."

"Have there been any holes dug in your yard?" Paige asked.

How could she know, thought Dylan. His face must have shown her that she was right as she went on. "It's like it's happening all over again. My brother was obsessed with finding the missing bones."

Dylan was listening to her words with great interest. This had happened before. Maybe he could figure out how to stop Caleb from becoming a monster. "What bones?"

Paige looked around nervously. "Not here. Too many people may be listening." She nodded to someone over his shoulder. Dylan turned around to see the guard from earlier watching them. "We could talk on the bus back to the school," he told her.

"It depends on if I will be able to keep my lunch down," she replied with a smile.

As they finished eating their lunches, JP and Terry sat down with them. They both looked as if they had been in the desert. Terry was brushing sand off his hair. "You two gone fossil digging yet? It's not bad as long as you don't have Neanderthals trying to bury you," said Terry.

"Josh and his little gang of future jail birds. He is such a jerk. He was mad because I wouldn't let him bury Ethan, so he buried us," JP said, shaking his head as if to get water out of his ears. "This place really needs some sort of hydration station. I'm burning up."

Terry wiped sweat from his face, which made him look even dirtier than usual owing to the fact that he had smeared mud on his cheek. "The smell is what gets me. I know that they want it to be realistic, but the tar smells awful."

"I can help you with that," Paige said as she pulled out a bottle from her purse. "I make it myself, strawberries and baby powder." She squeezed some white lotion from the bottle into Terry's hand.

He held it to his nose and sniffed, and then he rubbed his hands together. "I always have to smell great," she laughed.

"I think that you always smell good," Dylan said shyly. Both JP and Terry looked away from him, embarrassed. Dylan didn't care; he was enjoying himself. This had been a truly fun trip. Odd but fun.

Coach Sara was calling for attention. "All right, you lazy maggots, we are now going to be learning about a famous dinosaur. Please make your way to the *Spinosaurus* exhibit where our wonderful guide, Alex, will teach you something new. *Now move it!*"

Students started to move from the picnic tables. The four started walking when JP looked up and asked, "Weren't there three raptors?" He looked at Dylan, who said, "Told you, weirdness follows our school."

Dylan laughed. He saw Caleb get up; he was swatting away some mosquitos. The security guard that had been watching Dylan grabbed Caleb's upper arm. Right away Dylan knew that it was a mistake. Caleb started to scream as Dylan ran over to him. "Sorry, sir, he doesn't like to be touched. Is everything all right?"

The guard released Caleb's arm. "Didn't mean to frighten him, just didn't want him to get stuck." He pointed down at some tar that Caleb had almost stepped in. "Tar is the worst thing that you can step in; that's how many of these marvelous creatures met their makers. Now y'all run along. Learn about my friend the *Spinosaurus*. Oh, and don't forget to check out the *Triceratops*." He waved them off with a smile.

They all walked to the exhibit behind the fossil-digging sandbox. Dylan could see two large holes in the sand where JP and Terry had obviously pulled themselves out of the sand that Josh had buried them under. Dylan had not yet seen this exhibit. It was the only one that was not made of wax but true dinosaur bones.

Alex had begun speaking. "As you can see, behind me is the only constructed skeleton of the mega dinosaur known as the *Spinosaurus*. Archeologists have been able to recreate its skeleton almost completely. Notice that our dino is only missing two bones to make it complete.

Dylan took in just how large the dinosaur was; it would not have been able to fit in his house. It stood on its hind legs like a T-Rex. Also, like the T-Rex, it had two small arms coming out from its huge rib cage. On the end of each arm were sharp claws. The head was large and its snout was at least a foot long and filled with jagged teeth. They reminded Dylan of Caleb's x-ray.

Alex was pointing at the claws. "Those babies are two feet long and can cut through flesh like it was warm butter. The claws were only one of his many defenses; the tailbone shows us that he had a spiked tail and very good strength and balance.

Dylan looked closer at the tailbone. It had to be at least six feet long. He looked where Alex was pointing now. It was the bony spine coming out of the backbone. It looked like a huge fin. He continued to listen to Alex. "The fin is the most amazing part. It is believed that when the dinosaur came to the end of its life cycle, the body would pump blood into the fin, causing it to have a red glow."

Caleb came up to Dylan and kicked him. "What was that for?" asked Dylan.

Caleb didn't say anything. Instead, he pointed to the leg of the *Spinosaurus*. Dylan looked at the blue bone, wondering why it was blue.

Alex answered his question without having to be asked. "This skeleton is only missing two bones to make it complete. We have made fake bones to represent them. They are made of wax. You can see where they are by their blue color."

Dylan didn't need Caleb's second kick to understand. The blue leg bone was the same shape and size of the bone that Bonedigger had dug up from the backyard. The same bone that had disappeared earlier that day.

XI

The leg bone of a dinosaur had been buried in his backyard! He couldn't believe it. Dylan looked at the blue wax bone closely. Caleb was panting hard next to him. "You okay, bro?" Dylan asked him.

Caleb was transfixed by the dinosaur skeleton. "I think it's the same bone. Matthew says it is and that is bad. He says I am changing. I'm scared." He let out a deep breath.

Dylan could see tears starting in Caleb's eyes. "You shouldn't listen to Matthew. It doesn't matter now that the bone is gone." Dylan looked at the skeleton some more, trying to find the second blue bone. His eyes finally hit it; it was a lot smaller than the leg bone and was on the front of the snout. The bone was only about eight inches long and very sharp.

"If the leg bone was hidden in my backyard, could the other small bone be buried back there as well?" Dylan thought. Why had someone been digging holes in the yard? Were they looking for the leg bone? And what, Dylan now realized, was a horn bone? If they had found the leg bone in the garage, maybe the intruder thought the horn was nearby.

All this information was going through his head so fast that he barely heard Alex talking until he saw that Caleb was staring at him with rapt attention. "That is why this guy was not a fun dinosaur to meet on the way home." Alex was laughing at his joke. "Now here is what is so mysterious about our guy, Jack. He was found right here in Golfing Blue. He is the only fossil found here, and he was found next to something very odd." Alex paused as if to see if his audience would ask, "What was odd?"

Alex bent down and picked up a rock that was sitting next to the bone foot. "This here is a piece of tektite. It's extremely rare; the ancient civilization called the Mayans used tektite to make weapons. It is rumored that they also used tektite to cast spells. There was one spell that could even bring the dead back to life. There are three kinds of tektite—red, green, and blue. All three were found around Jack here. We had them on display until 1994 when the blue tektite was stolen."

Dylan mulled over this new information in his head. Why would anyone steal a rock from here? Why was the leg and horn not found with the rest of the skeleton? There were so many questions he could barely think straight. Looking up, he realized that Alex had finished his speech. Students were starting to walk off in different directions.

Caleb was still looking at the Spinosaurus. His eyes were fixed onto the blue leg bone. Dylan tapped his shoulder. Caleb jumped and looked into Dylan's face, and for the few seconds that their eyes met, Dylan saw a flash of red in his brother's eyes. Dylan stepped back. Caleb said nothing; he just turned and headed for the gift shop.

Paige took Dylan's hand. "Come on." They started walking along a dirt path. "Do you have any plans for tomorrow?"

Dylan went a little flushed. Was she asking him out on a date? "No, I don't have any plans. Why?"

Paige looked around. "Would you want to meet me for lunch? Maybe at the pizzeria?"

"Yeah, that would be awesome," Dylan said with excitement. "Would eleven o'clock work?" Dylan didn't get the answer to his question. Up ahead on the path he heard a familiar voice.

"You know for a dinosaur you sure are small, Terry Dactyl," Josh said as he pushed JP out of his way. He was with a couple of other boys who were laughing. JP picked himself up as Dylan and Paige came into view.

"Why don't you pick on someone your own size, Josh? You know, like Coach Manly," Dylan said it to get Josh's attention off Terry. However, it didn't work.

Josh grabbed Terry by the underarms and lifted him off his feet. "Hey, you know all dinosaurs are extinct except you, Terry Dactyl." He looked at Dylan and smiled. "Do you know how most of them died?" Terry was struggling to free himself. "They fell into tar pits." Josh finished as he threw Terry off the path. Josh laughed and motioned for his friends to follow him.

Once they were gone, Dylan called for Terry. Terry had been thrown into a part of the jungle that had been roped off. He was out of bounds, and if he got caught, he would be in major trouble. Unfortunately, Terry was already in major trouble. He was lying face up, not moving. Dylan didn't understand at first why Terry was not getting up. Josh had not thrown him that hard and it looked as if he had landed in a patch of soft mud.

JP looked nervous. "Should we find a teacher?"

Dylan's eyes filled with horror as he realized why Terry was not getting up. It was not that he didn't want to, he couldn't. It was not mud he had landed in. It was tar, and he was sinking into the black smelly substance.

Dylan didn't care about the rules; Terry needed help fast. Dylan jumped over the wooden fence, being careful not to step into the tar himself. "Hold on, Terry, I'm going to get you out of there."

Dylan saw the frightened look on Terry's face. He could see that Terry was trying to pull his arm up but was only making things worse. Dylan grabbed a tree branch and pushed one part of the branch into the tar where he had seen Terry's hand. "Can you grab the branch?"

Lifting his head slightly, he replied, "I can feel it, but can't get a good grip on it."

Dylan moved the branch a little bit to the left. "How about now?" Dylan saw Terry move his arm and a sudden tug on the branch told him that Terry had been able to get a good grip. Dylan pulled up, and slowly Terry's arm came into view. "Just stay calm," he said not only to Terry but to himself as well.

Dylan put the other end of the branch on the top of the wooden fence. JP and Paige grabbed it; they started to pull along with Dylan. With a squelching noise, they got Terry to his feet. "All right, try lifting your feet," Dylan instructed.

Terry, covered with the tar, tried lifting his leg. "My feet are in too deep. I can't pull them out."

Dylan looked around, "Okay, I'm going to reach in and pull your foot. When you feel me tug, start pulling up." Dylan got down on the branch that Terry was still gripping onto.

Being this close to the tar, it was hard not to get sick from the smell. Dylan plunged his arm into the muck. It was elbow deep by the time he found Terry's foot. He gave his foot a tug, but it felt as if the harder he pulled, the more it tried to pull him in.

Finally, after about five minutes, he got Terry's foot out. "Pull yourself up onto the branch," Dylan said. He had pulled his own arms out of the tar. Suddenly, the branch began to shake. Dylan grabbed hold so that he would not fall into the tar. He saw Terry struggling to hold on. The branch was in the air. Dylan saw the fence fly underneath him as the branch broke.

He felt Terry fall on top of him. Dylan rolled him off. The sun seemed to have been blocked out. Dylan understood why as he looked up at a hulking figure.

"What on earth were you two doing?" came Coach Sara's booming voice. "You are both going to have detention this afternoon for going out of bounds." She pulled them to their feet by the neck of their shirts. "You filthy boys. You will also help Janitor Jibby clean the bus tomorrow. The buses will be leaving for school in fifteen minutes. Don't miss it!"

As Coach Sara walked away, she gave JP and Paige an evil glare. Dylan and Terry were frozen in place. Both were breathing heavily. JP and Paige looked a little scared as they approached. "Are you two okay?" JP asked in a shaky voice.

Dylan nodded slowly as he rubbed tar off his arms. He felt so stupid; he should have told Coach Sara that it was all Josh's fault but, truth was, she wouldn't have cared anyway. Dylan looked at Terry. He was a lot worse off than he was; there was tar all over his clothes and hair.

They began to walk toward the gift shop. They stopped by the bathroom so that Dylan and Terry could try to wash some of the tar off. As they walked into the gift shop, Dylan noticed once again that the guard was keeping a close eye on him.

Caleb was standing in front of the shelf of puzzle boxes. Dylan wondered why he was interested in them. "What are you looking at?" Dylan asked.

Caleb turned, "These aren't like the one you have. The one you have is dangerous." He had a strange, scared look on his face. "You should have gotten rid of it! Now we are doomed." He walked out of the gift shop and to the buses.

"Well, at least we all survived the field trip," JP said.

Paige gave him a stern look. "We still have the bus ride back to the school."

Dylan took one of the puzzle boxes off the shelf, but he was not sure how to open it. He moved his fingers all over the box and heard a small click. The lid opened. It wasn't very deep, just big enough to hide small items like money or jewelry. "What is hidden in Mom's box?" he thought.

A large hand took the box from Dylan's hands. The security guard that had been watching him was looking at him through his sunglasses. "If you are not going to buy it, put it back."

Dylan quailed under the guard's glare. "Sorry, I was just looking at it." The guard didn't respond; he just pointed to the exit. Dylan followed the others out to the bus. He turned back to see the guard still staring at him. He got on the bus with the feeling of eyes on the back of his head. This field trip had been a strange one; he was just glad it was finally over.

The bus ride back had not been fun. The bus driver, Marty, had made a big fuss about Dylan and Terry being covered in tar. He said that he didn't want the bad smell to get into the seats. He also made them sit together in the very back seat on trash bags. This upset Dylan because he wanted to spend more time with Paige.

The bus bounced and sped down the road. Dylan was holding onto the seat in front of him, and the hot tar smell was not making it easy to keep his lunch down. He did not regret helping Terry, who had been whispering "sorry" in Dylan's ear ever since getting on the bus.

After swerving into a few mailboxes and almost hitting a tree, the bus jumped the curb of the school's parking lot and screeched to a halt. Once again, students grabbed barf bags as they left the bus.

Paige and JP were waiting for them when they got off the bus. Together, they walked up the steps to the school. There was only about an hour left before the end of the school day, but they were still supposed to go to class. So they headed up to Mrs. Ragoon's classroom.

Dylan was having trouble getting things to not stick to his arms. When he grabbed the doorknob of the classroom, Terry had to help unstick him. This didn't really help much because the hand that Terry used was just as sticky, so JP had to pull his hand off Dylan.

They sat down at their desks. Terry looked like he was having trouble; he was covered with the tar worse than Dylan was. Mrs. Ragoon walked into the room. Judging from the way she walked, a little wobbly, she had not totally gotten over the bus ride.

She sat down at her desk, pulled a metal container out of a drawer, and took a gulp. Dylan wasn't sure what the red liquid was inside, but some of it trickled down her pointed chin. Whatever it was, it brought her back to her normal self. "Get out paper and pencil."

She wiped the red liquid off her chin and licked her fingers. "I hope you all enjoyed the field trip. Were you taking notes?" Nobody shook their heads. "Well, this is an educational institution and note taking is very important. I want a three-page report on what you learned from our trip. It is to be handed in first thing Monday morning."

The class gave a loud sigh. No one wanted to do a report over the weekend. Dylan was worried that this would take away more time from Paige and his date for tomorrow. Mrs. Ragoon put the spelling words for next week's test on the board. Dylan copied them down; it took him awhile due to his sticky fingers.

The bell rang, and Mrs. Ragoon stood up. "Don't forget about your reports. Dylan and Terry, Mr. Hoggle is expecting you in detention but has asked that you both go to the showers first, and the nurse has a change of clothes for you, Terry."

They started packing up their bags when Paige came over to Dylan. "So are we still good for lunch tomorrow?"

Dylan was exploding with happiness; he had thought she was going to have second thoughts about it. "Yeah, it will be great." He tried to keep his voice casual, but it was hard to hide the excitement.

She smiled at him. "Bring that box. Maybe we can figure out the puzzle." She gave him a quick hug and left the room.

JP was putting his backpack on as he walked over to Dylan. He had a serious look on his face. "Hey, I've got to run. Don't want to miss the bus. Good luck tomorrow. Oh, and if you hear anything strange while you are washing off that tar, get out of there ASAP." He gave Dylan a high five, which got stuck for a few seconds as he headed for his bus.

Dylan and Terry headed toward the showers in the gym locker room. "This is all my fault. I am such a loser. I should have just let Josh finish me off," Terry said with a shaky voice.

Dylan punched him hard in the shoulder. "Don't say that. Josh is a jerk. Besides, you didn't ask him to throw you into the tar, and I helped you because you're my friend and because your aunt would have killed me."

Terry laughed. "Thanks. I better go get the clothes from the nurse. I'll be back." He walked away.

Dylan went into the locker rooms. He hated taking showers at school, but even he had to admit that the tar smell was making him sick to his stomach. He chose the very last shower. He undressed and put his clothes on the bench.

Dylan turned the hot water on and started to scrub his arms with the bar of soap. The steam rose all around and was filling the room. He was rinsing off when he heard a locker door slam shut. Sticking his head out of the curtain he shouted, "Terry, is that you?"

There was no answer. Dylan started shampooing his hair. At least he didn't smell like tar anymore. Once again, he heard a noise. He took a deep breath and let the water wash over him. He was letting what JP said get to him. The noises were probably just Terry, Dylan hoped. He turned off the water and grabbed a towel. He began drying off, when he heard a raspy voice saying, "Dylan,"

He turned his head toward the voice, but no one was there. "Anyone there?" he asked the room. The steam was still swirling around. Dylan put his clothes on and noticed that one of the other showers was going; it must have been Terry. Dylan looked into the mirror, shocked to find the words "DESTROY THE BOX" written in the steam.

The other shower turned off. Terry opened the curtain and walked out wearing a towel. He must have seen the look of horror on Dylan's face. "What's wrong?" he asked as he approached the mirror. He stared at the words. "Who did that?"

"I don't know," Dylan said. "Did you hear someone say my name?"

Terry gave him a look. "I didn't hear anything. But please don't leave me alone in here. I will get dressed quickly." He grabbed the clothes and went behind the curtain. A couple of minutes later he came out, wearing clothes that must have been from the sixties.

Dylan looked around; he could have sworn that he had heard someone call his name. He opened all the shower curtains and stall doors to see if anyone was hiding. Nobody else other than Terry was in here. They turned to leave, and Dylan knew that they were in trouble. Standing in the doorway was a man. A man with slimy green hands.

XIV

Dylan had heard stories about a strange green man that was sometimes seen in the school, but he had never believed in them. Now he was looking into the eyes of what students called the frogman. His slimy green skin made Dylan want to throw up. His eyes were bulging out of his head, and they didn't look as if they belonged so close to his ears. He was wearing a lab coat and tan slacks. He had nothing on his webbed feet.

Terry grabbed Dylan's arm. "Is that the frogman?"

There was no other way out. Dylan knew they were trapped. He wondered why the frogman was just standing there. He had all the power; Dylan and Terry were defenseless.

The frogman took a couple of steps. He looked strange; his knees stood out at an angle that seemed painful. His feet made a gross squishy noise as he walked. Dylan saw his green eyes looking over them. "This day just keeps getting worse," Dylan thought. "Now I am going to be eaten by the frogman."

The frogman got closer; Dylan didn't move as the frogman's head came within inches of his face. Dylan recoiled as the webbed hand reached out and touched his cheek. Dylan stayed still, waiting for the frogman's next move.

Dylan jumped as the frogman's mouth opened; he saw a long pink thing shoot out. Dylan fell into the lockers. He watched as the tongue wrapped around his backpack that he had left sitting on the bench. The tongue slowly brought the backpack to the frogman.

Out of nowhere came Terry's scream of rage. Terry tackled the frogman, and they both hit the floor. Dylan pulled himself out of shock and grabbed Terry's hand, pulling him to his feet. As the frog-man was pulling himself up, they ran out of the locker room.

They didn't look back. Unfortunately for them, they ran straight into Principal Schmitt. "Where have you two been? Mr. Hoggle is waiting for you in detention." She pointed an old wrinkled finger toward the detention room.

"The frogman attacked us in the locker room. He took my backpack!" said Dylan quickly.

Principal Schmitt gave him a searching look. "There is no such thing as the frogman," she said harshly.

Terry chimed in. "It's true, Mrs. Schmitt. There really is a frog-man. We were in the shower, then he attacked us."

"Get to detention now before you're there permanently." Her eyes flashed behind her spectacles. They knew that they would not win any arguments so they went on to the detention room.

As they walked in, they were surprised to see Sam sitting at a desk. What on earth could perfect Sam have done to get him put in detention? Dylan thought as he sat down next to him. Terry took the desk behind Sam.

Mr. Hoggle was standing at his desk in the front of the room. He was such a small man that Dylan could barely see his head over the desk.

"Welcome to detention," he said in a shrill voice. "You may leave at five o'clock. While you are here, you may work on home-work. The after school program has sent over a tutor if you need any help."

Now Dylan understood what Sam was doing there. He was not in detention; perfect Sam was there to help with homework.

"What took you guys so long to get here?" Sam asked. Terry told him about what happened in the locker room.

Sam looked amazed. "So there really is a frogman hopping around the school. That must have been scary. It's a good thing you got away."

"Yeah, but he took my backpack," said Dylan angrily.

"Well, maybe he will do your homework for you," Sam laughed. "You just better hope he gets you an A."

Dylan slammed his head into his forehead. "Stupid!"

"I didn't think my joke was that bad," Sam said, looking at Dylan with a worried expression.

"Not that. I just realized that my mom's box was in my bag. Now I will never know what secret it keeps." Dylan felt mad at himself for not grabbing the bag when Terry had knocked him over.

"Dude, it's not your fault. It sounds like he had you guys cornered. If you had gone for the bag, he might have been able to get hold of you," said Sam, trying to comfort him.

Dylan didn't want to hear it. He had half a mind to go back to the locker room and see if his bag was still there, but he knew that he didn't want to run into the frogman again.

Sam decided to change the subject. "So how was the ride with Paige?"

This took Dylan's mind away from his troubles for a bit. They didn't get any homework done. Instead, they sat and talked about the trip. He told Sam about the date tomorrow. Sam seemed happy for him. They took up the entire time talking. When Mr. Hoggle dismissed them, Dylan and Terry said goodbye to Sam and went to get their bikes.

As they approached the bike rail, Dylan noticed a silver Honda parked at the street corner. He looked closer and felt his stomach drop. Sitting in the car watching him through binoculars was the security guard from Dino Kingdom.

Dylan pointed out the car to Terry. They unlocked their bikes. Terry, sounding puzzle, asked, "What do you think he wants?"

Dylan was not sure why the guard had followed him back to school. Did he think that I stole something from the gift shop? Dylan thought. He felt uneasy as they began to ride their bikes home. He glanced over his shoulder; the car was moving. "Let's take a few extra turns. I don't want this guy knowing where we live."

Terry agreed and they sped up, going up a side street and then taking a sharp left turn. The car was still behind them. Terry pointed up ahead to the Hellman cemetery and said, "Let's go through here. He won't be able to follow us in the car."

They rode into the cemetery, flying past mausoleums and headstones. Even though the sun had not begun to set, it was much darker in the graveyard. The wind blew through the trees. Just like the school, this place was rumored to be haunted by ghosts and goblins. After the day he had, Dylan worried about what he might see if they stayed in here too long. The frogman had turned out to be real. What other horrors could the school be hiding?

Dylan's mind was racing just as fast as he was pedaling. He wasn't paying attention to the ground. A giant tree root was sticking out of the ground. Dylan hit it with such force that he flew off the bike.

He slammed face first into soft dirt. Terry stopped his bike and came over to Dylan. "You okay?" He helped Dylan up.

Dylan pulled his bike off the ground. He was getting ready to ride off again when he saw the name on the tombstone in front of him. It read, "Here lies a true hero. Nina Dactyl."

Dylan looked closer at the stone; there was no date of birth or death. It looked old and weathered. It looked as if graffiti had been written on it. He could make out the word "traitor" in what seemed to be faded black spray paint.

Dylan started to say something, but the look on Terry's face stopped him. He looked at the name on the headstone and he understood. "Was she a relative of yours?" he asked Terry.

Terry wiped tears from his eyes. "It was my mom," he said in a choked voice. "She died when I was little. I sometimes come here and talk to her."

Dylan didn't know what to say or how to comfort Terry. He had never asked Terry why he lived with his aunt. This made Dylan upset. Terry's mom had left him because she had died; Dylan's mom was still very much alive and she left because she wanted to leave.

Would Terry's mom have raised him if she had not died? Dylan was embarrassed by his feelings of jealousy. Terry could come and talk to his mom anytime; he knew where she was. Dylan had to wait for his mom to make a surprise visit for him to talk to her.

A sudden clanging brought Dylan back to reality. The security guard had started to follow them on foot. Dylan could see the beam of his flashlight moving through the graveyard.

"We have got to go," said Terry in a nervous whisper. Both boys got on their bikes and rode out of a side entrance to the cemetery. They were back on the street, pedaling as fast as their legs could go. They tried to stay in the shadows of the houses and kept looking back to see if the guard had followed them. They made it to Dylan's backyard and shut the gate.

Terry told Dylan good night and jumped the fence into his on yard. Dylan opened the back door and went inside.

Caleb was sitting on the couch. The TV was off, and the only light was coming from a small lamp sitting on the end table. "Matthew says that they are going to be angry. They want what is inside the box or they will hurt me," said Caleb.

Dylan's range of emotions was tiring; he was sick and tired of Caleb and his imaginary friends. Dad had left because of him and his issues, and maybe that was why Mom had not come back to see them. The anger inside him was rising up. "Just shut up, Caleb. I don't care what Matthew says. He is not real! That stupid box has brought me nothing but trouble, and I'm glad it's gone. Whoever is angry about it, they can go ahead and take you away. Maybe then Mom and Dad will come home and we can be a family again!"

The shock and hurt look on Caleb's face gave Dylan a feeling of satisfaction. Caleb got to his feet. His hands were clenched in fists. For a split second, Dylan was sure Caleb was going to punch him. Caleb puffed up his chest but then backed down. Dylan could see tears starting to form in his eyes. He was not surprised when Caleb ran out of the room. Dylan heard his brother's door slam shut.

He felt a little ashamed of his outburst. He turned on the TV and watched a couple of his favorite shows. Caleb did not come down to watch with him. It was almost seven, and he was getting hungry. He pulled out the leftovers his grandmother had left in the refrigerator. He made a plate for him and Caleb. He called for Caleb to come down, but he didn't come.

Dylan was eating alone when his grandmother came in from work. He didn't feel much like talking. He finished his chicken nuggets and told his grandmother good night. He headed upstairs when he looked out of the living room window and saw the silver Honda sitting across the street.

How had it found him? he thought. They had been very careful about watching their backs. He locked the front door and headed up to his room. Caleb was coming out of the bathroom. He was wearing his pajama shorts and no shirt. They looked at each other for a few minutes; neither of them wanted to speak to each other. Caleb started scratching his arm. Dylan noticed that he was scratching a rash. It was red and seemed infected. Dylan took a closer look; the rash looked like scales. The more Caleb scratched the rash, the worse the skin seemed to get.

Dylan went into the bathroom and got some anti-itch cream. He handed it to Caleb. "Try putting this on it." Caleb took the ointment without saying anything and went back to his room.

Dylan, feeling guilty about what he had said, went into his room and got ready for bed. He looked outside; the silver car was still there. Was it going to stay there all night? What did he want? Was it the box? Well, if that is it, he didn't have it anymore. But was that a good or a bad thing? He was not sure anymore.

Dylan woke up the next morning around nine thirty. He had not slept well. He stretched and yawned. Then he remembered the silver car. He slowly peeked through the blinds, looking out at the bright morning. He searched up and down the street for the car, but it was gone. A rush of relief came over him.

He got ready for the day, as he had to be at school by two so that he could help clean the buses with Janitor Jibby. He was not looking forward to it, but at least he would get to meet with Paige beforehand.

He walked downstairs; he was going to apologize to Caleb. Caleb, however, had gotten up early and gone bike riding, according to his grandmother.

"May I have twenty dollars?" Dylan asked. He wanted to pay for both his and Paige's lunch.

His grandmother gave him a stern look. "Now why do you need money?" She was dusting off the TV. "I still haven't seen you clean up your room."

Dylan didn't really want to talk about his love life with her. How gross was that? She was too old to understand love. He really wanted the money so he did what he had to do. "I'm meeting up with Paige for lunch. She is going to help me with a report that I have to do."

His grandmother gave him a searching look. Dylan tried to keep his mind off of how beautiful Paige was, but his grandmother seemed to see through his facade. She smiled. "My little man is growing up. I think I might cry." She stopped dusting and pulled Dylan into a hug. "I guess I could float you a twenty. As long as you go clean up your room. Also, I don't know what happened between you and Caleb last night, but when he gets home, you should try talking to him. He seemed really sad this morning."

Dylan scarfed down a couple of slices of toast then headed to his room to clean it. Cleaning his room took quite a while, but he got most everything shoved into his closet or under the bed. As long as his grandmother didn't open the closet doors, the room looked good. He turned off his bedroom light and ran down the stairs, taking two at a time.

He was hoping Caleb would be home before he left, but he was still out on his bike ride. He took the twenty-dollar bill out of his grandmother's hands and even let her kiss him on the cheek. He raced out the back door and petted Bonedigger, who had been lying in the grass, sunbathing. He hopped on his bike and headed for the pizzeria.

It took him about fifteen minutes to bike to Michelangelo's pizzeria. He put his bike in the back and locked it to the lamppost. The bell rang over the door as he pushed it open. The restaurant was owned by a man named Phil H. He was a jolly man who was obsessed with making new pizzas.

Dylan looked around at the four-seated square tables. He saw Mr. H through the window in the wall that divided the kitchen from the dining area. He waved and Dylan waved back. Mr. H had lived in Golfing Blue forever, and he was always willing to listen to the kids' strange stories. He wore a blue apron that was always covered in flour and bits of dough. His balding head still had a little bit of red hair in the front.

He saw Paige sitting at the table in the front corner. He walked over and sat down. "Hey," he said excitedly.

Paige was rubbing lotion on her hands. "I'm so glad that you were able to come. I thought that you might have been in trouble after the whole detention thing."

"Naw, my grandmother is cool." He left out the small fact that he had not told her. He pulled the menu closer so that he could see the specials. "So what kind of pizza are you in the mood for? The duck a l'orange sounds interesting, but I have never had the turtle and rabbit pizza either."

At that moment, Mr. H came to the table. "If you are looking for a healthy pizza, might I suggest the split pea pizza or the eggplant and pepperoni? Both are brand new to the menu." He had a very calm and soothing voice.

Paige looked at him. "Those sound lovely, but I think we will have the mighty meats meat lovers. I just love the taste of all those meats put together." She handed him the menu.

Mr. H took it and gave a little bow. "Very good choice. I will get it in the oven for you right now. Is there anything else that I can do for you?"

"Could we get a couple of fizzy colas? Please?" said Dylan.

"Right away, my friend." Mr. H left to get the drinks. Dylan was not as nervous as he had been the other day. They talked about how it was so unfair that they had to write a report over the weekend and about the crazy bus driver, Marty.

A little while later, they were drinking and eating. Paige put down her slice of pizza and asked, "Did you bring the puzzle box?" She took a sip of her drink.

Dylan had totally forgotten that she wanted to see it. He explained about how the frogman had attacked him and took his backpack and about the mysterious words on the fogged up mirror. To his surprise, she did not seem shocked to find out that the frogman was real. Instead, she said, "Do you think there is any chance of getting it back?"

Dylan thought on that for a moment. If he were to be honest with himself, he didn't really care to get the box back, especially if that meant he would have to face the frogman again. "I don't know how. No one knows where the frogman lives."

"Of course they do," said Mr. H, coming to the table. "He lives in the elementary school. Not exactly sure where, but he normally finds you." Dylan gave him the money for the pizza, and Mr. H took the empty plates. "You two have a wonderful day."

Five minutes later, they waved goodbye to Mr. H and started to walk up the street. They stopped at a magnolia tree and sat beneath it. "I need to tell you something about my brother," said Paige. "If I do, please don't laugh at me or think I am crazy."

"I won't laugh at you," said Dylan sincerely. "You can tell me anything, I got attacked by the frogman so I think I may even be crazy." He was hoping that she felt safe enough to tell him what had gotten her upset.

Paige took a deep breath. "My brother was studying the dinosaurs and he came across some old hieroglyphs. He thought they were spells. He believed that an evil presence was trying to bring back the dinosaurs so they could rule Earth." Paige took a breath. "My brother started to change. Strange things started happening. He became obsessed with trying to find the two lost bones of the *Spinosaurus* and the stolen tektite. He said that the job had to be done to save our race."

Dylan was mulling it over in his mind. Could something sinister be hiding at Dino Kingdom? Why did that guard follow him and what happened to the missing bone?

Paige continued. "He started breaking out in rashes one night; he even peeled off his skin like a snake. Then he said he knew how to fix things and went to Dino Kingdom, but he never came back." She had tears rolling down her cheeks. She brushed them away with the back of her hands. She looked Dylan in the eyes and asked, "Will you help me?"

Dylan thought about it for a second, then replied, "Yes."

XVII

Dylan was not really sure how he would be able to help her. It did occur to him that what happened to Paige's brother was possibly happening to Caleb. Dylan may not always get along with him, but he felt bad for what he had said the night before. Not to mention, his grandmother would be angry if he became a monster.

Dylan took Paige's hand and gave it a squeeze. "What do you want me to do?" He wanted to give off a sense of bravery, but deep inside he was terrified. He was only a ten-year-old boy. What could he do against something supernatural?

Paige slowly grinned. "Thank you. Everyone else I have told just says that I'm going through depression." She opened her purse and pulled out a small blue notebook. "My brother left me this and told me that it would explain everything, but it just gives me more questions."

Dylan took the notebook and flipped through the pages. It was rough sketches of different dinosaurs. On some of the pages were handwritten notes about the skin and claws. As he looked at the pictures, he became aware that most of the drawings didn't resemble those of the wax figures at the Dino Kingdom.

"Your brother must have been studying for a long time to be able to get all of this information," Dylan said as he came to an entry entitled Spinosaurus. This page was filled with notes that spilled over onto a second page. It noted where each bone of the large skeleton at Dino Kingdom was found with the exception of the two missing ones.

He looked closer at a small note scribbled next to the large bone that Bonedigger had dug up in the backyard. It read, "Security guard knows." Dylan took a deep breath. Could he have been talking about the guard that had followed him home?

This was getting scarier by the minute. Had the guard been the person who broke into the garage and took the bone? If it had been him, what had made those claw marks? All these questions made Dylan's head spin.

"What do you think your brother wanted to do in the park?" Dylan asked. "I don't know anything about magic."

"I think that he was trying to put the *Spinosaurus* back together. It's the one he was most interested in. He came home one night saying that he was close to finding the missing bones. He was positive that they were somewhere in Golfing Blue." Paige pushed her hair out of her face.

"Well, there's only one bone missing now. The leg bone was in my backyard. Bonedigger dug it up, but it was stolen out of my garage." Dylan wiped sweat from his forehead.

"I wonder who buried it in your backyard?" asked Paige, taking back the notebook.

Dylan thought about it for a minute in silence. "My mom used to dig holes in the yard. My grandmother told me just the other day. Maybe that's how she found the puzzle box."

Paige turned back to the pages on *Spinosaurus*. "Maybe, but the box is too small to put the bone in. I don't see how the puzzle box fits in with anything else, other than it was bought at Dino Kingdom."

Dylan sighed. "You're right. I don't have any clue. I was never able to even get it to open." He stood up and stretched. "Even so, I don't know where the box is now. Do you think that the frogman wanted the box?"

Paige gave him a thoughtful look. "I don't know what he would want with it unless it has magic powers. We need to get that box back."

Dylan had a feeling that she was right. He wasn't sure why, but he felt that the box held answers. Not only answers about what was going on with Caleb, but also why his mom didn't love him anymore.

Maybe the frogman had left the bag in the locker room. Could they be so lucky?

"I can sneak in and look for it," Paige said hurriedly. She looked at the notebook and put her hand on the page. "It's what my brother would want me to do." She wiped away more tears.

Dylan, wanting to show that he was brave and sensitive, wiped a tear from her cheek "I'll do it; I have to go to the school anyway." Dylan looked at his watch. "It's almost two, so I will go over there and clean the buses, then I will find the frogman." Dylan sounded braver than he felt. "If anything happens to me, you can finish what your brother started. You can help Caleb from having the same fate." He took a deep breath as if his next words were hard to say aloud. "And if I don't make it back, tell Caleb I'm sorry and I love him."

Paige looked worried but, trying to calm his fears said, "You will be fine. You are strong and can take on anything. I will do more research to see if I can find out anything else about the missing bones and the piece of tektite."

They walked back to the pizzeria and Dylan got his bike. "I will call you later tonight." He swung a leg over the bike. Paige stopped him and gave him a kiss on the cheek. "For good luck," she told him. Feeling as if angels were singing, he rode off to the school, sure that he was going to succeed in finding the box.

XVIII

Dylan arrived at the school as Terry was locking up his bike. Dylan jumped off his bike and locked it to the bike rack. Dylan must have had a worried expression on his face because Terry asked, "Everything all right?"

Dylan looked around to make sure nobody else was around. "I'm going to find the frogman and get that box back."

Terry stared at him with a horrified look. "Are you insane? Why do you want to go looking for trouble?" Terry grabbed his arm. "It's crazy. Why do you even want that box? Don't you remember the writing on the mirror?"

Dylan knew that Terry was right. This whole thing had become so crazy. The thought of being Paige's hero crossed his mind; maybe that was why he was so keen on helping her. That was part of it, but also it had a lot to do with his mom. "I just have to."

Terry let go of his arm, "I'm not going to let you do this." He paused and shut his eyes. "Not by yourself anyway. I'm going to help you." They began to walk. "I saw Janitor Jibby heading to the playground with a big metal barrel. Let's go get the buses done, then we can figure out our next move."

Dylan was happy that Terry was with him. He may not have been good friends with him, but he felt that he could trust him. They walked onto the playground; they passed the swings and the seesaw before finding the janitor.

Janitor Jibby was an older man and moved extremely slowly. He was wearing his usual uniform, an old looking tan jumpsuit. His name was embroidered in red on top. It looked as if that was his only clothes. He had black hair that went around the sides and back of his head, but the top was all grey. He wore a belt that had the strangest key ring attached. It looked like one of those old dungeon key rings made of iron and had at least two hundred keys on it. Dylan always wondered what all the keys went to, but he never had the courage to ask.

They approached him as he was pouring chunky yellow goo into the sewer grate. "What is that stuff?" Terry asked, making a disgusted face.

Dylan was not sure of Janitor Jibby; it looked like he had cotton balls growing from his large ears. Dylan waved at the janitor to get his attention. Janitor Jibby stopped pouring and looked up at them. "You two must be the boys here to wash the buses. I was just finishing up feeding time." He patted the metal barrel. "Everyone loves mac and cheese."

Dylan was not sure what he was feeding in the sewer, but he didn't really want to know. He had enough mystery and strangeness in his life at the moment.

The janitor took off his gloves, revealing old, wrinkled hands. His fingers shook slightly and nails were black as soot. "Well, I guess you two had better get started with the buses. Now you will want to make sure to use warm water. They get angry if they are cold." He led them to the back parking lot. There were four buses parked, and they looked as if they had just gone mudding.

Janitor Jibby brought them a couple of large buckets and some wash towels. He handed Dylan a mop. "Don't forget to wash the wheels. If you need me, I'll be in my office. Let me know when you get done." He walked hunched-backed into the school.

Terry and Dylan grabbed the towels and started to work. "So how do you plan to find Mr. Froggy?" Terry asked as he scrubbed mud off the bus tires.

"Once we get done with the buses, I'm going to go to the locker room and look to see if he dropped it. If not, I'll have to figure out what to do next," Dylan said as he mopped the windows. He was thinking that the frogman probably hadn't dropped it in the locker room, but he didn't know where else to start.

If they thought that it would not take long to clean four buses, they were mistaken. It was almost five o'clock before they got done. The buses seemed not to want to be cleaned. Every time they got one bus done, Terry would find spots that they missed. The bus would also make strange noises if they scrubbed too hard.

Terry had just finished the windshield on the last bus. He threw the muddy towel into the water bucket. "All right, so are we ready for this?"

Dylan nodded and wiped his muddy hands on his shirt. "Let's get this done." They quietly walked into the school. Janitor Jibby's office was to the left, but the locker room was to the right. They went down the hallway. Each of them kept looking over their shoulders to make sure Jibby had not noticed them.

They made it into the gym; they could hear a loud noise coming from Coach Sara's office. Terry pushed the door open just a little. "Coach Sara is sleeping on the chair," he whispered.

They started to make their way to the locker room. Dylan thought that the school looked creepier when nobody was around. Dylan opened the locker room door and peered into the room. It was dark and foreboding; he put his hand on the wall searching for the light switch. He found it after a few seconds, and the lights slowly came to life.

Dylan looked around, but he didn't see the box or his bag. He checked underneath the benches and in the showers but found nothing. He looked at Terry. "I don't know what I was thinking. He probably took them somewhere else in the school." He felt defeated. How was he going to find the frogman, and if he did find him, how was he going to get the box from him?

Terry was opening the unlocked lockers. "Maybe we should ask Janitor Jibby. He's been here since before dirt." He shut one of the locker doors, and it made a loud clang. The noise echoed through the room.

A loud bang came from the gym. Terry quickly turned out the lights. A voice rang in their ears. "Who's out there? Show yourself!" Coach Sara had woken up, and it sounded like she was not in a good mood. "I know you're here somewhere. No one is supposed to be in here."

Dylan could hear her walking around the gym. He saw the look on Terry's face. Dylan understood why he was scared; he was just as scared. Coach Sara was not a person to forgive rule breaking, and being inside the school when it was supposed to be locked was definitely against the rules.

They backed deeper into the locker room. It was so dark that they had to feel their way against the wall. Coach Sara had made it to the rope that hung in the center of the gym; she must have been shaking it because they could hear the bell at the top ringing. They knew the only way out of the locker room was through the door, and they would get caught for sure.

"What are we going to do?" whimpered Terry. His voice filled with terror. "Do you think she will just go back to sleep?"

"Doubt it," said Dylan in a whisper. He could hear her footsteps, or that might be the beating of his heart. Dylan knew that there was no escape. As soon as she opened the door and turned on the light, they were busted.

Dylan felt Terry's arm; they had run out of the locker room. He felt the shower curtain. Grabbing Terry, Dylan pulled him into the shower area. He pulled the curtain shut just as the lights came on. Coach Sara was breathing heavily as she lumbered into the room. "Where are you? I was having a good dream about crushing little brats and you woke me up."

A little confused by her question, Dylan pushed back against the shower handle. He heard a tiny click from behind. He had to hold his hand over Terry's mouth so that his cry of surprise was muffled. A small crack in the wall revealed a secret door. Dylan pulled it open; it led to a dark tunnel.

Coach Sara was banging open stall doors, still searching for them. The tunnel looked foreboding. Terry gave him a look that plainly said anything is better than being caught by the coach. They entered the tunnel, and Dylan slowly shut the door. Immediately, he knew he had made a mistake. The second that it shut, they knew that they would not be able to get back out because the door had locked.

Dylan pushed on the solid wall, but it didn't budge. Panic was starting to bubble in his stomach. He had made the decision to enter the tunnel. At the time, it seemed like the best idea, but where did this tunnel lead? Even worse, what might live at the end of the tunnel?

Dylan felt around the damp wall. The darkness was overwhelming; he tried taking deep breaths to calm the panic. He felt something squishy and heard a moan. "Is that you Terry?"

"Yeah, you poked me in the eye. I can't see anything," came Terry's reply.

Dylan felt for Terry's hand. "Let's stay together." They started walking down the tunnel. After about five minutes of walking in the dark, Dylan saw a small light up ahead. As they drew closer, Dylan could make out a small door. "What do you think? Should we open it?"

"We have come this far, might as well," Terry said.

With a trembling hand, Dylan pushed the door open. Light flooded the tunnel; it took a few seconds for their eyes to readjust. They slowly walked in and looked around.

Dylan felt like he was in the science lab. There were diagrams of animals being dissected and little cages sat against the wall. Sitting on a wobbly wooden table were yearbooks and pictures of students. Dylan looked at an open yearbook; it was dirty and torn in the corners. The students' pictures had red X marks over some and question marks over others.

Terry pulled his attention to the corner of the room. "Someone must be sleeping in here." He was pointing to a filthy mattress on the floor. It had a dirty sheet crumpled on top of it with a torn brown teddy bear lying on it.

Dylan kicked the mattress; a couple of cockroaches scurried out from underneath. "Who would want to sleep in here. It's disgusting." He picked up the teddy bear by the arm. Its head was only attached by a few stitches; it flopped to the side.

The other tables were littered with old newspapers and broken glass. There were jars filled with bad smelling, different colored liquids. Dylan picked up a jar with dark red goo in it. "I think this is blood."

The door slammed from behind them. Dylan and Terry slowly turned to find themselves face to face once again with the frogman. He stood in front of the door they had entered; his white lab coat fluttering as he made a hopping movement. His eyes were filled with shock. He had not expected to find someone in his room. He turned the bolt, locking them in, green slime dripping down the doorknob.

Dylan looked around; there was a second door to their right. Dylan tapped Terry on the foot. Dylan noticed that the frogman's eyes were glued to him. If they ran for the door, they wouldn't make it. Dylan's only thought was to get Terry and himself out of this mess.

Dylan was so preoccupied with trying to get to the door that he didn't notice the sudden movement. The frogman jumped and landed inches from Dylan. For a split second, he saw fear in the frogman's eyes. The green, slimy hand roughly grabbed the teddy bear out of Dylan's hand.

An involuntary scream came out of Dylan's mouth. The frogman hugged the bear close to his chest. With eyes focused on Terry, the frogman slammed the bear onto the table in between them. They both jumped. Dylan thought that at any moment his heart would burst from his chest.

The frogman pulled a sharp piece of broken metal out of the pocket of his coat. He grabbed Terry's arm and put it onto the teddy bear. The frogman leaned over. Dylan saw a look of terror on Terry's face. He was expecting to hear Terry's screams of pain, but they never came.

The frogman straightened up. Terry's arm was free. The frogman put down the metal piece and held up the bear. He had put the head back on. He gave it a big slimy kiss and began his hopping motion and hugging his teddy bear.

Dylan suddenly understood why the frogman had shown fear. He was scared that Dylan was going to hurt his teddy bear. Dylan was not sure what to do. The frogman was not attacking them, but why lock them in?

Dylan decided that he was not going to be afraid. "I want my backpack back. What did you do with it?" Dylan was not sure what to expect; he was not even sure if the frogman could speak.

The frogman gave him a searching look, then turned so quickly that it made Dylan's head spin. He pushed Terry against the wall, putting his green webbed hand against Terry's throat. Dylan thought that the frogman was going to bite Terry's ear off, but then realized that he was whispering in his ear.

Terry fell to the floor, breathing heavily. The frogman had released him and hopped over to his bed. He just stood there staring at them. Then he pointed at the unlocked door. Dylan helped Terry up. They both looked at him; Terry rubbed his throat. Dylan had had enough. "Where is my backpack?"

The frogman sat down and started to play with his bear. Dylan knew that it was hopeless. Whatever happened to his bag, the frogman was not going to be of any help. He was more worried about Terry than getting it back anyway. "Let's go before he changes his mind." Dylan helped Terry to the door.

It turned out that the door led to a hallway of more doors. Dylan wasn't sure which one to take, so he just picked the first door that opened.

They were back inside the school, the first-grade hallway by the looks of it. Terry took a deep breath. "That was insane. I thought he was going to kill me!"

Dylan ran his hand through his hair. "But we still didn't find my bag." They began walking to the front doors. "We had better go tell Jibby that we are done," Dylan said as they turned the corner. They stopped in midstep. They were standing in front of Principal Schmitt.

"And what are we doing here at this time on a Saturday?" Her voice was crisp and sharp, but she had not yelled. Her eyes rolled over them. Neither of them could speak. "Well, since the cats have your tongues, I will let Mr. Jibby know that you are leaving."

Both boys found their voices and began to speak at the same time. "Yes, ma'am, thank you Principal Schmitt."

They started to walk when the principal grabbed Dylan's shoulder. She pulled out from behind her back Dylan's backpack. "Do not leave your stuff just lying around the school, please." She handed him the bag.

Dylan took it; not believing his luck. He and Terry took off running as fast as they could toward the doors. They didn't look back as they went to their bikes. They climbed on and sped off. They didn't slow down until they got to their street. Dylan took his backpack off and opened it up, "Everything is here, including the box." He pulled out the box, put his hand back in, and pulled out a book. "This yearbook is not mine."

He turned the yearbook over and saw that it was from the year 1988. "This is from the year my mother was in fifth grade. I wonder why someone put it in my backpack."

Terry took the book from Dylan, giving it a look of dislike. "I don't know why someone would put that in your bag but . . ." Terry was cut off by the sounds of police sirens. A police car drove by quickly. "I wonder what has happened," said Terry.

Dylan looked closer at the police car. It had pulled into his driveway. They hurried to the house. Dylan got off his bike as his grandmother came out the front door. "What's going on?" Dylan asked, concerned.

His grandmother's eyes were filled with tears as she said, "Caleb is missing. The police found his bike in the cemetery. The wheel had been torn off." His grandmother pulled him into a hug as tears started to roll down his cheeks.

The police officers didn't leave the house until about nine o'clock that night. Dylan was lying in his bed. He could not sleep. His grandmother had gone into her room, but he could hear her crying through the thin walls. He got up and quietly went into his brother's room. Bonedigger was lying on Caleb's bed. Dylan sat down and started to pet him.

What had happened to his brother? He thought. He felt that this was all his fault. Caleb would not have gone for a bike ride if I had not said such mean things to him. I wish I had just left the stupid box alone. He looked down, trying to fight back the tears. There was some weird paper on the floor. Picking it up, he realized that it was not paper at all. It was skin, like a snake would shed.

He looked at it closer; it was about the same size as Caleb's arm. He remembered what Paige had said about her brother shedding off his skin before he went to Dino Kingdom. He took the skin back to his room and pulled the puzzle box out of his bag. He looked at it with determination. He was going to figure out how to open it even if it took all night.

He spent almost an hour and a half just turning it over and over in his hands, pushing everywhere he could think of, but nothing worked. He started studying the pictures around the box. All the eggs in the nest were painted green except for one big one painted blue. It reminded him of the blue-skinned *Dilophosaurus*. He put his finger on the blue egg and pushed. Nothing happened; he turned to the side with a circle with three scratches through it.

Looking closer, he saw that there was some blue in the carved circle. Dylan picked at it. Under his fingernail, he saw a blue paint chip. Maybe it was painted blue at some point. He pushed on it, but once again, nothing happened. He looked at all the pictures again. If any of them had had color, it had been chipped off from years of aging.

A thought occurred to him. Maybe, if he pushed both the egg and the circle, it would unlock. He tried and heard a click, but it didn't open. What was the click? He looked once again at the pictures. One of them must have been painted blue, but which one? He saw the sun and the moon. If the drawing between the two was supposed to be earth, shouldn't it have been painted blue?

He put his forefinger on the blue egg and his thumb on the circle with the scratches. He heard the click once more. Taking a deep breath, he pushed on the earth picture. The top popped open. Dylan was so shocked that he almost dropped the box.

He pulled the top all the way open. There was a page of notebook paper folded into a square. Under that was a blue shard of glass. "The stolen tektite!" Dylan shouted, before he could stop himself.

He walked to his door and listened for his grandmother's footsteps, but there was only silence. He went back to the bed and unfolded the piece of paper. It was in his mother's handwriting.

> ND,
>
> Thanks for sharing your secret with me. Your friendship means the world to me. I will always keep this part of the tektite triangle safe. You were right about the leg bone. I have buried it in the backyard. Mom was a little annoyed with all the holes, but she will get over it. I know that Mr. B will never give up trying to find this, so I protected it by locking it in this puzzle box.
>
> The spot where I buried the horn is in the cemetery. The true hero will protect it. Mr. B won't be able to dig it up without exposing him-

self. I hope that this helps you; you deserve to have a good life.

XOXO
Judy

Dylan finished reading the note. So many questions were going through his mind. His mom had really stolen the tektite. Who was ND? Had she ever read this note? Or did this note become lost and forgotten just like the puzzle box?

His mom must have really cared about this person. More than she cared about me, Dylan thought. If this helps me get my brother back, I will do whatever it takes. He had to find the last bone. Maybe this Mr. B will trade for it.

Dylan reread the letter over and over. Who is the true hero? He thought about it but couldn't come up with anything. Maybe there was some clue on the box. He looked at the carved pictures and it hit him. He looked at the circle with the three scratches. He had seen it before, just the other day, and it explained the identity of the real hero. He knew where the last piece of the puzzle was hidden.

He picked up the phone, forgetting about how late it was, and called the number Paige had given him. She answered on the second ring. "Hello."

Dylan was exploding with excitement, "I solved the puzzle. Meet me at nine in the cemetery!"

XXI

It was almost one in the morning before Dylan's mind let him fall asleep. He dreamed that someone in a black hood had come into his room. The hooded figure was searching for something but couldn't find it. The smell of the intruder was rancid; it was the same smell that he had smelled in his mother's room the other day.

His alarm clock woke him up at eight. He turned it off without hitting the snooze button once. He was too excited to worry about his dream. He didn't even realize that the smell still lingered around his room. He got up; he was not even going to bother with taking a shower. There was too much work to be done.

He put on a grubby pair of jeans and an old sweatshirt that belonged to his mom. He emptied his book bag of all his school supplies. He grabbed the puzzle box from underneath his pillow and put it into the bag. Pulling on his shoes, he stumbled down the stairs and into the kitchen. He made a few peanut butter and jelly sandwiches and packed them in his bag. He grabbed some chips and some candy bars and shoved them in the bag as well.

He climbed back upstairs and opened his grandmother's bedroom door. She was still sleeping; he didn't want to disturb her. If he woke her, she might try to stop him from going to find Caleb. He was not sure what waited for him, but he was sure that he had to try.

Shutting the door quietly, he went back downstairs. He scribbled a quick note telling his grandmother that he loved her and that things were going to be all right. Bonedigger was lying on the sofa. Dylan took him by the collar and hooked up a leash. Bonedigger seemed to understand that what Dylan was doing was important because he patiently waited for him to grab his bag. They left the house out the back door so that he could get his bike.

Dylan was halfway to the cemetery; he had to ride slowly so that Bonedigger could keep up, when Terry caught up to him. "Hey, Dylan, so why did you need me to come to the cemetery with you?"

Dylan slowed down a little. "I think I know where the last bone is buried." He had wanted Terry to come with him because of what he might have to do. He hadn't told Terry everything when he called him the night before. "Did you bring the shovels?"

Terry gave him a worried expression. "Yeah, I got them here in my bag." They reached the cemetery gates and pushed them open. They left their bikes at the entrance.

Dylan led the way. "Grandma told me that the police found Caleb's bike by an old oak tree in the cemetery. I think that somehow he figured out where the bone was and tried to get to it before anyone else could."

They were walking with gusto. "Do you think he found it?" asked Terry concerned. "Do you think that is why someone kidnapped him?"

Dylan nodded. "I think my mom and her friend were trying to hide the bones and the tektite from a guy named Mr. B." He explained about the letter he had found in the puzzle box.

They came to the tall dark oak tree. Dylan was nervous about hurting Terry's feelings but he had to move fast before someone else figured out where to look. "Terry, I think I know who ND was." He was slightly worried that Terry might be upset about bringing it up, but he continued on. "I think it was your mom."

Terry looked at Dylan with shock. "My mom! You think ND is my mom?" Terry seemed to be trying to control his emotions. "Do you want to dig up my mother's grave?"

Dylan was afraid that Terry would stop him, but he had to make him understand. Dylan was facing Terry as Paige walked out from behind the tree. "What's he doing here?" she asked.

Dylan took a deep breath. "Let me explain please. Then if you want to hit me, I will not stop you." Terry looked angry as his fists were clenched. He looked at his mom's tombstone. "Explain."

Dylan took the fact that Terry didn't punch him as a good sign. Both Terry and Paige were giving him an "Are you insane?" look. He held tight to Bonedigger's leash; even the dog seemed to be listening with anticipation. "The note said that the true hero would protect the bone. When I was looking at your mom's tombstone the night I crashed, I saw that it said she was a true hero." He pointed to the words on the stone. "I then realized that my mom and your mom would have been the same age. So ND could have stood for Nina Dactyl." He pointed out the name. "But the most convincing evidence was the 'o' in the word 'hero.'"

Paige and Terry gave a puzzled look as they looked at the "o" in the word "hero." There were three small scratch marks going through it. Dylan pulled the puzzle box from his backpack; he showed them the side of the box. "It's the same drawing." Dylan looked determined. "The other bone is buried somewhere around here."

"And you think that this Mr. B will trade your brother for this bone?" Terry asked. Dylan noted that Terry's voice was calm and understanding. Dylan thought that maybe it was pity.

Paige's face showed deep thought. "Mr. B. That name is in my brother's notes." She pulled out the blue notebook and flipped through a few pages. "Yes, here it is. It doesn't say much, just a small note under the drawings of the *Ankylosaurus.*"

She handed the book to Dylan. He looked at the picture and read the little note at the bottom of the page aloud. "Mr. Big or Mr. B leader." Dylan was not sure what it meant by "leader."

"Leader of what?"

Paige shook her head. "No clue."

Dylan turned back to Terry. "Bonedigger was able to dig up the leg bone. I'm hoping that he can sniff out the horn bone." Dylan was aware that he was asking a lot from Terry. He hardly ever spoke about his mom and now was being asked to help dig up the dirt around her. "Did you happen to bring that yearbook? Maybe we can look at it and see if our moms were in the same class?" Dylan asked Terry because in all the commotion last night, Terry had left with the yearbook still in his hand.

"No, sorry, I forgot about it. But I believe you and if it will help get Caleb home, I will do what we need to do." He had tears in his eyes. He wiped them away and took Bonedigger's leash. "One condition; you treat me like an equal in this. I don't want to be left in the dark because you don't want me to get hurt."

Nodding, Dylan agreed. They let Bonedigger sniff around the ground. "Even if we do find the bone, what's the next move?" asked Paige.

Dylan sighed. "We need to figure out what happened to the leg bone." He scratched his head. "Then we need to sneak into Dino Kingdom and wait for the park to close. I bet that's when this Mr. B will come out."

Paige thought about it for a second. "We could go in like we are visiting the park, then hide in the woods until closing. Maybe we will find both of our brothers there." Bonedigger was still sniffing the ground.

Dylan looked at her and smiled. "I bet you anything that the guard that followed me home has the leg bone. He was probably trying to see if I had the tektite or the horn bone. So Mr. B will already have the leg bone I think."

Terry looked up from the tombstone. "You're probably right. I wouldn't be surprised if it was the guard who grabbed Caleb." Bonedigger was tugging on the leash. "Paige, you should go on to Dino Kingdom. If there is anything strange going on, it will give you more time to find it. We will stay here until we find the bone."

Dylan nodded his agreement. "But be careful. We don't want the guard to get suspicious." Paige gave him a hug. "You are so brave, thank you." She kissed him on the cheek. Terry made a gagging noise. She gave him a sharp look. "I will be waiting for you at the gift shop." She handed Dylan her brother's notebook. "You keep this just in case you need it. I already have it memorized." She turned and walked off.

Dylan pulled out the sandwiches from his bag. "You hungry?" He offered Terry a sandwich. Terry took it. They sat and ate but stopped abruptly as Bonedigger started to dig in a small patch of flowers. Terry and Dylan grabbed the shovels and started helping Bonedigger. They dug about four feet down before finding a small rectangular metal box. They dug around it trying to pry it from the ground. They finally pulled it out. They were hot and sweaty. Even though this had been Dylan's idea, he could hardly believe that he was on the right track. The wind blew through the trees. The air carried a foul smell. Dylan looked around; they were the only two people here. What was that smell?

Terry pulled a screwdriver from his bag. He was trying to pry the rusted box open. After a few minutes of twisting and pulling the screwdriver, the box popped open with a loud noise. They both stared into the box. A mixed look of disbelief and happiness spread over their faces as Dylan picked up the horn bone.

I t took Dylan and Terry over two hours to ride their bikes to Dino Kingdom as Bonedigger had slowed them down. He didn't want to stay in the backyard, so Dylan had to put him inside. Once they arrived at the park, it was almost closing time. They went in through the gift shop hoping that they looked as if they were just visiting.

Dylan found it unnerving that there were no security guards around this time. But then he noticed that the gift shop was empty; there was not even a cashier. Terry must have been feeling like Dylan was as he said, "Where is everyone?"

Dylan gave him a puzzled look. "I don't know, but I don't like it. Paige should have been here by now." He was getting a sinking feeling in his stomach. What if something had happened to her? What if she had been locked up somewhere with Caleb?

Dylan looked up and down all the aisles to make sure that nobody was hiding. "Maybe they are using the bathroom," Dylan said as he pushed the boys' room door open. No one was there; the place was empty.

Terry was standing at the security guard's office door. "It's locked. He must be outside somewhere." He took a salt rock lamp off the shelf and slammed it into the doorknob, breaking it off. "What? We are already breaking laws," Terry said at Dylan's look of shock.

"I wasn't thinking about having a criminal record until I was at least fifteen. Although at the rate my life is going, I might not even make it past fourth grade," Dylan said, exasperated as he followed Terry through the door.

There was nothing extraordinary about this room. There were monitors all around the walls, each showing a different part of the park. Once again, he felt uneasiness about the fact that not only was the gift shop empty of employees but the park was void of visitors. He was looking closely at the screens; not a single person out there. Then a movement on the third screen caught his attention.

"Look here." Dylan pointed to the screen. He was looking at the raptors once again and there were three of them. The two that were made of wax looked like they always did; the third, however, looked like it was looking straight at him through the camera.

Terry looked at the screen as well. "I don't remember that middle one being there. He looks so real." They were staring so hard at the screen, as if something was going to jump out, that they both jumped when they heard a knocking on the closet door.

Dylan tore his eyes from the monitor. They walked to the closet, afraid of what might be behind the door. Dylan turned the knob and pulled open the door. A body fell out of the closet. They screamed as they looked at the man tied up lying on the floor.

It was the tour guide, Alex. Dylan saw that the lenses of his glasses had been cracked. He reached down and felt under his nose. "He's still alive. I can feel his breath." Dylan turned to Terry, "What should we do with him?"

After a few minutes of arguing, they decided that it was safest to just untie him and push him back in to the closet. Alex was a lot heavier than he looked, so it took both of them to put him back. Terry dropped his book bag to help.

A movement caught the corner of Dylan's eye. He turned back to the monitor. The two wax raptors were knocked over. Terry was watching the screen in silence. The raptor in the middle had its mouth open. Wasn't his mouth closed a minute ago?" Dylan asked, not truly wanting the answer.

They kept their eyes on the dinosaur. Both boys fell backward as the raptor lunged at the camera. Dylan knocked Terry's book bag over and the old yearbook slid out. Dylan gave Terry a questioning look. "You saw that dinosaur come to life, right?"

Terry had bent down to pick up the yearbook. "Yeah, I saw it." Terry was trying to shove the book back into the bag without Dylan noticing.

It was too late. Dylan stopped Terry from zipping up his bag. "I thought you said you forgot to bring it? Why did you lie about the yearbook?"

Terry seemed to be having an argument in his own head. "Please don't be mad, but . . ." Terry didn't have time to finish his sentence. A loud rough voice came from the main gift shop room. "He is in here somewhere. Lock the doors."

Terry threw his backpack on, and he and Dylan exited the office. Dylan could see the two security guards at the front locking the doors that led to the parking lot. Their only hope now was to go out into the park. Dylan pointed to the doors and nodded at Terry.

Terry shook his head and mouthed the word "Dinosaurs."

Dylan could see that he was scared, and so was he, but they had no other choice. "We have to. We have to save my brother." Dylan could see the determined look in Terry's face.

Terry took a breath and said, "Okay, so how do we get over there without the guards seeing us?"

Dylan thought about it. The guards were starting to check the aisles. He looked at the shelves behind him. They were filled with different colored tektite lamps. An idea struck him. "Get ready to run for the door." He lifted up the lamp and threw it into the air. It soared straight through the open office door. Dylan heard it crash on the office floor.

His plan had worked. Both guards looked at the office door. "He must have broken into the office," snarled the guard that had followed him home. Both guards were running up the center aisle toward the office.

Both Dylan and Terry made a break for it; they ran up the aisle at the far end of the store. They made it to the doors. Dylan saw the guards go into the office. He pushed open the door, and they sneaked out.

The humidity in the park immediately made Dylan sweat. He pulled Terry up a path and jumped behind some trees. "What are we going to do now?" Terry said. He was looking through the trees.

Dylan understood what he was searching for, the guards or the raptor that was running loose. Dylan was hoping not to have a run in with either. He pulled out the notebook and started flipping through it. "There has to be a second exit out of here." He found the page he was looking for, a map of the park. He took his finger and found the gift shop; he followed a line that ran all around the park. He knew thirty-foot walls surrounded the park, but he was looking for a marker indicating a door.

He could not find one. According to the map, the only way in and out was the doors in the gift shop. There was a rustling in the trees. Both boys turned and watched as a head started to poke out of the bushes. It was not one of the guards' heads or the raptor; it was a *Stegosaurus*. Dylan yelled, took Terry's arm, and pulled him back onto the pathway. "I must be going insane. I think that there are live dinosaurs in this park."

Terry pulled on Dylan's arm to slow him down. "We can't keep running blindly around. We won't be able to find the gift shop if we stray from the path." Terry didn't seem as scared of the *Stegosaurus* as he had the raptor. "We need to make a plan to get out the front door before those guards find us."

"A little late for that," the guard said as he stepped out from behind a tree. He grabbed Terry and tossed him onto his shoulder. The second guard restrained Dylan and frog marched him down the path.

They struggled with their captors, but the guards were abnormally strong. They were in front of the *Spinosaurus* skeleton. The guards put Dylan and Terry in a standing position and made them face the skeleton.

Underneath the large dinosaur was a black hooded figure. He stood at least twelve feet tall; the black cloak covered his entire body. The two guards bowed to him without letting go of the boys while saying, "We have them, sir."

The hooded figure clapped what looked like his hands. An icy chill ran down Dylan's spine as the cloak fell to his wrists and revealed that he did not have human hands but two claws. His talons were sharp; he used them to pull off the hood. Dylan stared in shock. The figure was not human at all. He was a dinosaur!

As Mr. B walked toward them, Dylan was horrified. "Welcome to my home," Mr. B said. His voice was deep and had finality about it. It was also very proper as if he had gone to school for years to perfect it. "I'm so glad that you were able to join us for this historic night."

Dylan and Terry had stopped struggling and had not even noticed that the guards had released their arms. Fear was spreading through all of his bones. Dylan pulled up the courage to interrupt Mr. B. "What have you done with my brother?"

Mr. B must have not been expecting Dylan to be brave. He dropped his tone. "I'm sorry. Do you not know that it's impolite to interrupt someone while they are speaking?" He gave a grin that showed sharp teeth. "I would suggest that you show me some respect. That is, if you would like to see your brother in one piece. It's been hard, but nobody has taken a bite out of him yet."

The guards laughed. They had removed their hats to reveal three horns on their heads. Dylan looked closer at Mr. B's head; he had seen a dinosaur with the same rocklike skin covering its face. He noticed that there were spikes coming out of his neck. "You're all dinosaurs." Dylan said.

Once again, the guards laughed at him. "Of course, we are. This is Dino Kingdom after all. What did you expect?" The guard hit him in the back. He fell to the ground.

Mr. B helped him up; Dylan could feel the scaly skin of his claws. "Now, now, that is no way to treat our guests. As I was saying, welcome to my kingdom. It seems that you have something that I want. Give it to me, and you and your friends can leave."

Dylan knew in his heart that this was a lie; he had to think of something fast. "Why do you want it?" Dylan really didn't care about an answer; he was just trying to stall for time.

Mr. B removed his cloak. Going down his back were plates that seemed to work as a shield. "At one point in time, my friend, my race was the dominant one. However, when the Neanderthals came along, they brought diseases. Most of us died out from illness; the dust from a big rock that hit earth millions of years ago smothered some. It was when we were on the brink of extinction that a great leader rose up and saved us."

He pointed to the skeleton. "The great *Spinosaurus*. He found a way for us to adapt and live in hiding. We learned the magic of the earth. He created this land for us to live on. He left the sanctuary of our walls to find food, but he was attacked and killed by the humans."

Dylan was only half-listening; he was trying to find a way to get away. However, Mr. B had them at his attention as he continued, "Now, with all the bones, we can revive him and exact our revenge on the Neanderthals."

Dylan stepped forward. "Okay, I have the horn. I will trade it for my brother." Dylan was not sure if he was making a smart choice, but he had to try.

Mr. B gave Dylan a searching look. "Your brother for the horn? And what about the tektite?" A flash of red in Mr. B's eyes told Dylan that there would be no trade. Dylan shouted, "No!" Mr. B grabbed Terry by the neck and began to choke him.

"Please stop. I will give you the horn. Just please put him down," Dylan said, worried that Terry's neck could have been snapped at any moment. He reached into his bag and pulled out the horn. The guards, which Dylan had concluded were Triceratops, took it out of his hand.

Mr. B lowered Terry to the ground but did not let go of his neck, then said, "Where is the tektite?"

Dylan could see that Terry was trying hard to catch his breath. His face was turning purple. Dylan could barely understand what Terry was saying. "Don't give it to him. He will take over the world."

Mr. B was not a patient individual. "No more stalling, give it now!" He threw Terry into a large tar pit. "Watch as your friend sinks to his death. Then you will either give me the tektite or watch as your brother shares the same fate."

Dylan looked at Terry. He was lying face up in the tar, his body lifeless as the tar slowly covered his body. Dylan, not knowing how he was going to help Terry, pulled out the puzzle box. "Please help him. Don't let him sink."

Mr. B watched with a joyful smile as Terry sank deeper into the tar. "Take it out of the box." Dylan couldn't hold back his tears as Terry's face slowly disappeared beneath the tar.

Terry was gone; Dylan couldn't move. It was his fault as he was the one who had pulled him into this mess. How was he going to tell Terry's aunt that he was gone? Mr. B was probably not going to let him live anyway. Also, what had happened to Caleb? Was he still alive, or had Mr. B already gotten rid of him. His thoughts moved to Paige. He really wanted to help her; now she was gone. The mystery of what happened to her brother was never going to be solved.

The snarling voice of Mr. B broke through his thoughts. "Take it out of the box!" He stomped his feet. "I do not want to have to hurt you, but I will."

Dylan was not sure if it was bravery or stupidity that made him speak. "Why don't you take it out yourself?" He found that his voice was filled with anger. Mr. B had killed his friend and probably his brother. He was sure that he was going to die as well, but he wouldn't go down without a fight.

Mr. B was getting annoyed; Dylan could hear it in his voice. "Go get the little brother, and tell the raptor that dinner will be served soon."

Dylan had heard what he needed to hear; Caleb was still alive. "No wait, I will open it." He held up the box, and putting his fingers on the buttons, he popped it open. The blue tektite gleamed in the moonlight. The guards looked at each other but didn't move.

Mr. B moved closer; he lowered his claws and picked up the tektite gingerly. "I, the last of the ankylosaur, will be granted the highest honors by the great king of the dinosaurs." He moved back to the skeleton; the guard that had been holding Terry took him the horn bone. Mr. B took off the blue wax piece and placed the bone in its place.

"You still don't have the leg bone! You'll never find it," Dylan said, hoping that they would not catch that he was lying. If they were able to bring the *Spinosaurus* back to life, the whole city would be destroyed.

Dylan's heart sank as Mr. B pulled out the leg bone from a bag. Mr. B smiled. "Now what were you saying that I would never find?" He carefully exchanged the blue leg bone for the real one. He approached the skull. "When the moonlight shines through the three tektites, it will breathe life into our savior." He held the green piece of tektite up at the moonlight.

The tektite started to glow; the guards were staring at it in awe. Dylan heard noises coming from the jungle; he turned his head to see the raptor that had jumped at the camera come into the light.

Mr. B placed the green tektite into the skull's right eye socket. "Come, my friends, witness the rebirth of your king!" He took the red tektite and held it up to the moonlight. It too started glowing. He placed it into the left eye socket.

Dylan watched as other dinosaurs came out of hiding. The guards had seemed to forget that he was even there. Dylan remembered how to get back to the gift shop, but the raptor was standing in the pathway. He looked around casually to find another escape, but the only way was straight into the jungle. If he left the path, he might get lost out there. He was also still determined to find his brother.

All the dinosaurs were watching with excitement as Mr. B was chanting over the final piece of tektite. Dylan knew that his time was running out. Any moment now, Mr. B would be finished and Dylan would be in deep trouble. He saw a spot in the wooden fence that he could duck under.

He took a small step. No one said anything. He took a slightly bigger step; still the guards didn't notice. Mr. B raised the blue tektite into the air. Dylan saw the moonlight hit it as he reached the fence. Quickly, he ducked under and hid behind a large tree.

Dylan peered through the branches; none of the dinosaurs had seen him leave. They were all too transfixed by Mr. B, who was still holding the blue piece of tektite in the moonlight. Nothing was happening; the tektite didn't glow as the other two had. Mr. B turned it so that the moonlight could hit it at a better angle. Still, nothing happened; the guards looked worried.

"Maybe it needs more time," said one guard. Dylan had slowly started to creep away from the tree deeper into the jungle and away from the skeleton. He could still hear the angry shouting from Mr. B. "*Made in China!*"

Dylan knew that he had only seconds before they noticed that he was gone. He felt in his pocket for the real tektite to make sure that it was still safe. He began to walk faster as Mr. B's voice carried on the wind. "It's a fake! Where did that little brat go? He must have the real one. Get him! The ceremony must be completed by midnight!"

Dylan broke into a run. They might not have known which way he went, but it would not take long to track him down. He had no clue on what to do next. He felt so alone, but he was not going to give up. He was going to be brave. He ran as fast as he could, jumping over fallen tree trunks. He noticed that there were more tar pits and tried his best to zigzag around them.

Deeper and deeper into the jungle he went. For a split second, he thought he had lost his pursuers. Then he heard them again. He was moving so fast that he didn't notice the ground sloping downward, and he fell. He got up, and his muscles were aching. He ran further; the voice of the guards rang in his head.

He was so excited that he didn't see the large tree roots sticking up out of the ground. He tripped, and landed in the mud. He could hear the two guards talking, saying something about someone named Slayer and then they left. That is when Dylan realized that he had not fallen into mud, but a tar pit.

Dylan was sinking fast. He knew that there was no way out. He wondered if Terry had felt the same fear as he sank. And he didn't even save his brother. He was a failure. The tar was so thick he knew that his body would be lost forever. His one comfort was that Mr. B would never be able to bring the *Spinosaurus* back to life. The blue tektite would be forever lost in the tar pits.

The tar had reached his neck; he was already getting light headed from the pressure on his chest. He could move his head. He saw a figure out of the corner of his eye. He tried to call for help, but the tar was strangling him.

The figure moved closer to him. He thought that he must have been imaging things. Paige was standing over him. He could see that she was saying something, but the tar had covered his ears. He tried to push up with his feet, but it was as if something was holding onto him and dragging him down. He smelled the tar as it went over his nose. His last image was of Paige as he slowly shut his eyes and darkness surrounded him.

Even though his head was now completely beneath the surface, he still had the sensation of sinking further down into nothingness. The darkness was peaceful. He slowly gave into death.

Hands were rubbing his face and body. Rough hands. He didn't know what was going on. The fingers were going up and down over him. Was this heaven? It was still dark, and he was having trouble opening his eyes. The hands were moving faster; he was starting to feel air in his lungs.

Something was cleaning out his nose and ears. He felt a different pair of hands on his face, wiping off the tar from his eyes. These hands felt smooth, not like the others. Dylan was finally able to open his eyes all the way. His vision was still a little blurry, but slowly Terry's face came into focus.

Dylan couldn't speak; not only because of the tar in his mouth but because he was in shock. After a few minutes of staring blankly, he spat and asked, "Are we dead?"

Terry gave a sigh of relief. "Almost. I was not sure if we were going to be able to pull you down fast enough. I was afraid that you would suffocate." He wiped more tar from Dylan's ears.

Dylan looked around, seeing who the other hands belonged to, and understood why they were so rough. They belonged to dinosaurs! There were at least five. He was not sure what type they were, but they all stood tall and had what looked like duckbills for mouths.

Dylan coughed, but most of the tar had gone. "I saw you die. Mr. B threw you, and you didn't move. How is this possible?"

"There are underground tunnels all over the park. We were hoping that Mr. B would have thrown you into the same one," answered Terry.

Now that Dylan was more alert and sure that he was not dead, he could see that they were all standing in a large cave. "But he didn't throw me in."

"And that is why they had me standing by." The squeaky voice came from behind. "I saw you run into the jungle. I confused the guards into thinking that you ran past me. I tried to catch up with you, but you fell down the hill. I saw that you were stuck and went to inform Slayer."

Dylan turned to see who was talking. He was surprised to see the raptor standing there. "You were going to eat my brother."

The raptor licked his lips and replied, "I do not deny that I am a carnivore. But I try my best not to eat humans. My name is Raspberry. I was given the name by a very special friend."

Dylan was having trouble getting his mind around everything. "So you knew that the dinosaurs were real, and you didn't tell me?" he asked Terry.

Terry looked upset. "I shouldn't have lied to you, but I'm going to tell you everything. Please just give me the chance. Afterward, if you never want to speak to me again, I will respect that." Terry pulled his backpack off; he reached in and pulled out the old yearbook. "You were very clever about figuring out your mom's puzzle box. It was me that wrote the message about destroying it on the locker room mirror."

Dylan stopped him. He was beginning to wonder if Terry was a good guy or if he had been playing him the entire time. "So did you have the frogman attack me?" he asked.

Terry looked startled. "No, no, I didn't even know that the frogman was going to be there. I just wanted you to destroy the box so that the blue tektite would be destroyed. I was as afraid of the frogman as you were, especially when he told me that he was going to tell you my secret."

Anger was starting to flow through Dylan once again. "What secret?" he asked.

Terry handed him the old yearbook. "You were right about almost everything, except for the initials ND. They didn't stand for my mom. That is what your mom used to call me, before we came up with the name Terry." Dylan looked at the page of the yearbook. He saw his mom's picture, and a few pictures down, he saw Terry's secret. Terry's picture showed him smiling; the name under the picture read Terry Dactyl.

"How is this even possible?" Dylan asked.

A voice that he didn't recognize spoke. "I can answer that."

He turned to see a dinosaur standing on his hind legs, wearing a leather jacket that had spikes sticking out of the back. Dylan knew that he was a Stegosaurus. His tail dragged behind him, and he wore gloves over his claws.

"You may call me Slayer. This is my area of the park. Now, to answer your question about my friend Terry here. He is made of wax. When the park was first built, the owners made wax figures of all the dinosaurs of which they had knowledge. They also made Neanderthals; that's why your mom would call him ND. They made a family of four—a man, woman, and two children, a boy and a girl.

When we found the park, the idea was that we would blend in with the wax dinosaurs."

Slayer stretched out his tail as he went on. "Some of us were fine with that, but others were not happy with being driven into hiding. They tried to take over. They killed the owners. That is when the ones of us who were not power hungry built the wall around the park in order to keep in the others. They heard the legend of the *Spinosaurus*, and Mr. B has been obsessed with it ever since."

Dylan was focused now on what Slayer was saying, but he still didn't understand how Terry was a part of it all. Slayer continued. "Mr. B took some of his followers and went out to find all the bones of the *Spinosaurus*. Then he found the tektites. He wanted revenge on the humans so he brought Terry and his family to life."

Dylan looked at Terry; he had tears rolling down his face. Terry had lived next door with his aunt for as long as Dylan could remember. But he never saw a dad or a sister.

Terry spoke softly. "He brought us to life with the tektite. He tortured us for years, and then he killed my dad and sister. My mom didn't want me to go the same way, so she sneaked me out of the park with Slayer's help. We lived happily for years, but then Mr. B found out where we were. Mom made a wax doll that resembled me. She sat the house on fire and when Mr. B's henchmen came, they saw her and what they thought was me melting. That's what is buried in her coffin. That is why your mom called her the true hero."

Terry wiped tears from his face. "I had no one for years, then I met your mother and she was nice to me. She kept my secrets and helped me to go to school. Then came her field trip to Dino Kingdom, I was scared to come back. What if they recognized me? The only one who did was Slayer. He told me that Mr. B was still searching for the bones, but two were missing. Your mom and I found them. While she was on the field trip, she stole the blue tektite."

"She saved the lives of many," chimed in Slayer.

"And she gave me my name," Raspberry, the raptor, said.

Terry looked at Dylan. "She was my best friend, but I knew that she would grow up and I would stay the same. After I completed the fifth grade, I would hide for years. Your mom grew up and went off on other adventures. When I saw that you were going to be at Hellman Elementary, I decided to go back."

Terry gave a smile. "It was nice not to hide anymore; no one remembered the kid from years ago. I was able to manipulate my wax to make it look like I had aged just a little bit each year, so nobody would get suspicious."

"Why on earth would you want to go through school a second time?" Dylan asked. He was losing his anger.

Terry laughed. "The years with your mom were some of the best years of my life."

Even though Dylan was thrilled that Terry was not dead, he still had his brother on his mind. "What about Caleb? I think that Mr. B might be turning him into some kind of dinosaur. I saw his x-rays at the dentist."

Terry took a breath. "Mr. B definitely has your brother, but you saw my x-rays. The dentist mixed them up. We don't think that Caleb is turning into a dinosaur."

That was a relief for Dylan, but the problem was that, dinosaur or not, Caleb was still in danger. "Do you know where he is?" Dylan asked.

The dinosaurs were shaking their heads. "Mr. B has him hidden," said Raspberry. "We don't know where he is."

Yet another new voice echoed through the cave, but this one Dylan recognized. "I know where he is. I found him." Dylan turned and gave Paige a huge smile.

XXVI

Paige had a torch in her hand as she approached Dylan. "I saw you sinking. I tried to get you out, but you were too far gone." She hugged him. "Mr. B has everything he needs to bring the Spinosaurus back to life. We have to get our brothers and get out of here."

Dylan was still smiling. "He doesn't have everything." He pulled the blue tektite from his pocket.

Terry gasped. "I thought you gave it to him."

Raspberry looked at it. "So this is why it exploded earlier when he was trying the ceremony."

Dylan put it back into his pocket. "When we were in the gift shop, I replaced the real one with one of those fake salt lamps. I was not sure if it would work, but I had to try."

Slayer gave a loud cheer. "My people only wish to live in peace. I will not say that I have not had to fight, but I do not wish to keep on with this war. We must make sure that this tektite does not fall into Mr. B's hands. It must be destroyed!"

Paige shouted, "No, we might need it to save our brothers. You can't destroy it until afterward!" She gave Dylan a frightened look.

Dylan was struggling with all of the new information about Dino Kingdom. He looked at Slayer, remembering what the two guards had said about not wanting to go into Slayer's territory. They were afraid of him. Why? There were so many questions that still needed to be answered. "Why are the other dinosaurs afraid to come into your area?" Dylan was not trying to be rude, but he felt that he needed a reason to believe him.

Slayer lowered his head. "You have every right to ask me that question. You see, humans have gotten things wrong about some of us. For instance, they believe that the *Tyrannosaurs Rex* was the king of the dinosaurs. This, however, is not true. The *Tyrannosaurus Rex* was a kind and loving creature. He would have never hurt a fly. Besides, how could he with those tiny arms? He was just so cute! Anyway, the true king was the *Stegosaurus*. In fact, I was the reigning king when I brought my people here. We were going extinct. I thought that by bringing together all dinosaurs that we would have a better chance of survival. I brought the Spinosaurus. He was crazy and so power hungry. I killed him. This is why some of the other dinosaurs fear me. They believe that I will kill them to put myself back in power."

Terry patted Slayer's hand. "We all make mistakes, but we must learn from them." Terry stepped up to Dylan. "I told you that I would help get Caleb back and I meant it. I hope that you can forgive me for not being honest with you from the beginning."

Dylan nodded. "What do we need to do to get to Caleb?" He may not fully trust Slayer or Raspberry yet, but as he looked into Terry's face, he knew that he could trust him. "Do these tunnels run all around the park? Is there one that could get us past the wall?"

Raspberry shook his head. "The tunnels do not go past the walls. The only way in and out is through the main gate. But maybe it's time for us to all stand against Mr. B. I can rally the rest of us who do not want to continue under Mr. B's regime."

Paige was looking nervous. "But what about our brothers? The tunnel I came through will lead us right back to them. We have to help them."

Dylan felt that this was the best way for him to rescue Caleb. "Slayer, can you please help us free my brother?"

Slayer bowed his head. "I will do anything to help the son of our human friend, Judy. My followers will go top side and attack. That should give you ample time to free your friends. Terry, you go with them. Once this battle is over, we can live in peace."

Terry nodded. It felt good to be back with his two friends, Dylan thought. The three of us can do anything if we stick together. Slayer sent the duckbill dinosaurs up one path, and Raspberry headed for a path on the left after he had given Dylan a smile and a nod.

Terry took a stick off the floor, and lit it on fire with Paige's torch. They began to walk away through the passage from which Paige had entered. The further they walked, the narrower the path got. Soon, they had to walk in a single file line while hunched over.

Dylan still had a lot of questions going through his head. "Why didn't you meet us in the gift shop?" he asked Paige.

She came to an abrupt stop, and Dylan crashed into her. This, in turn, caused Terry to crash into him. Paige turned her head; her beautiful green eyes mesmerized Dylan. "I got chased by the security guards."

Dylan could see a light up ahead; the tunnel was widening out again. They started to walk. Dylan could see the mouth of the tunnel, which meant they would soon be out in the open. He stopped, and again Terry bumped into him. "Sorry," Dylan said as he helped Terry straighten back up. "I think we need a plan. Even if the dinosaurs are all fighting, Mr. B is sure to leave at least one guard to watch Caleb."

Paige stopped and turned around. "You might be right. If he thinks you have the tektite, you will be the one he goes after." She pushed a strand of blond hair from her face.

The moonlight from the end of the tunnel was shining on her. Dylan could not help but notice how pretty she looked, but he had to stay focused. "That is what I mean. If there is a guard, he's sure to go after me first. That's why I should not be the one with the tektite. I think Paige should carry it. That way it will be safe. Terry, you can figure out how to get Caleb and Paige's brother out of whatever is keeping them trapped."

Terry looked nervous. "I will bring them into the tunnels and keep them safe." He turned to Paige. "Would you happen to have some of that lotion? The tar smell is making me nauseous."

Dylan took the tektite out of his pocket. Paige took it and placed it carefully into her purse. She handed Terry the lotion bottle. Dylan was staring at her again. She was beautiful; her skin was so smooth and shiny. She must have really liked that lotion. She said that that was what kept her skin so smooth. Dylan continued to fantasize about when this was all over, they would be able to go out on a real date and not have to worry about anything else. They began to walk to the tunnel's exit.

Paige's hair flowed in the small breeze from the wind blowing into the tunnel. Her hair was perfect, too perfect. Dylan and Terry were covered in mud and tar, but Paige was very clean. If she had been hiding, surely she would have gotten a little bit dirty. Dylan felt a nagging at his brain, but he couldn't figure out why.

They were almost there; Dylan could smell the night air. "You never told me your brother's name," Terry said to Paige.

She smiled and replied, "Oh, sorry, his name is Al."

They were inches from the exit. Dylan stopped; a strange look came over his face. Suddenly, he realized what the nagging feeling was trying to tell him. He grabbed Terry's hand and lifted it up to his nose. "Strawberries and tar with a hint of baby powder." It hit him like a train. He had smelled the same smell outside the window of his mom's room and right before Sam had been pushed into the trashcans. He had even smelled it at the cemetery.

He turned to face Paige; she had a huge grin across her face. She had the tektite in her hand. "I have always called him Big Al," Paige said as Mr. B took the tektite from her hand.

"Welcome back," he said as the two *Triceratops* guards grabbed him and Terry.

XXVII

Mr. B and the guards led Dylan and Terry out of the tunnel. "Dylan!" came a frightened voice. Dylan saw a cage with Caleb inside it. He was still wearing his pajamas; they were torn and dirty looking. His hair was a mess; it had clumps of mud in it as well as sticks stuck in the tangles.

"What have you done?" Dylan was struggling to break free and get to his brother.

Mr. B responded, "Nothing yet."

Dylan looked at Paige for the first time with disgust. "Have you been working with him the entire time?"

Paige ran her fingers across Dylan's face. "Oh, I have been working with him ever since I was born. You see, I was the only one who could leave the park. I had to get fresh meat. I've been doing it for years; this year the plan was to bring your friend Sam to the park. He's so great looking and a perfect meal for us, but then I saw you with your mom's puzzle box. I had tried to steal it that morning from your house. I would have if your idiot brother had not been trying to scare you. So I had to find a way to get you to be my bus buddy, I decided that I would feed the spiders. That way, he would be out of my way. Then things just fell into place. I told you that my favorite dinosaur was the *Dilophosaurus*."

Dylan felt three claws on his face; her hands had changed. The skin on her neck was loosening, and she pulled at it. It was just like the crest on the wax *Dilophosaurus's* neck. Her face elongated into a snout with bumps all over. Her skin was turning blue; she was becoming a *Dilophosaurus*.

"You see the crest was not used as camouflage like humans think. It is used for transforming." Claws busted out of Paige's shoes. "I'm so glad you are so easy to fool. I was the one who switched the dentist's x-rays. I was the one who put it into your brain that your little brother was becoming a dinosaur. I went into your house and left some of my dead skin so that you would think he was shedding."

Dylan saw that they were back in front of the Spinosaurus skeleton. The tektite pieces in its eyes were still glowing. Mr. B was holding the blue tektite in the moonlight. This time it was working. It started to glow. "You and your brother will make a nice snack for him when he wakes up. And don't worry, Neanderthal, I will resume your torture once you watch your friends die."

Dylan felt the earth shaking beneath his feet. Was it an earthquake? Mr. B turned around to face them. He looked stunned. "We must hurry. Slayer and his followers are on the way!"

The ground was really starting to shake. The guards, holding Dylan and Terry, were having trouble keeping their balance. Dylan gave Terry a glance, and they both threw their weight onto their captors. The guards went down; Dylan and Terry got to their feet.

Dylan ran over to the cage holding Caleb. "I'm sorry for all that I said to you the other night. You're not worthless and Mom didn't leave because of you. You will always be my brother, and I will have your back." Dylan was talking fast; he was not sure they would make it out alive and he had to tell him how sorry he was.

Terry was pulling on the bars. "We need a key." He tugged on each bar to see if any were loose. Dylan saw a flash of blue as Terry went flying. Paige had hit him hard with her tail. "Looking for this?" She held up the key. "If you want it, come and get it." Dylan charged at her; she must not have been expecting him to be so strong. He jumped onto her back and wrapped his hands around her neck. She lost her balance, and they fell in the dirt. He was punching her in the side. He was angrier than he had ever been. She had been his first true crush, and she wasn't even human. He had risked his life and the life of his friend and brother, all because he thought she was pretty. He felt stupid; he knew that he had smelled her lotion before. He should have known that she was a liar. With every punch and kick, he felt vindicated.

He tore the key from her claw. "Terry, catch!" Dylan shouted as he tossed the key high in the air. Terry caught it, and went to work on getting Caleb out of the cage. He saw that there was more fighting going on. Raspberry had tackled one of the guards. There were other dinosaurs fighting near the tunnel entrance and in the jungle.

Slayer had also joined in. He had a large sword, and he was circling the skeleton. Mr. B was on the other side holding a mace. In his concentration of what the others were doing, Dylan lost track of his own fight. Paige's claws slashed his chest; he felt the blood trickle down his stomach. He fell to the ground. Paige had malice in her eyes; she was going in for the kill.

Dylan watched as she raised her claws to strike, when a scream got his attention. "That's my brother!" Caleb came running and hit her in the side. It gave Dylan just the right amount of time to get up. He joined Caleb and Terry. "We have to keep him from completing the ceremony. After midnight, it won't work."

Even as he said it, he saw Slayer fall to the ground; his sword just feet from him. Mr. B slammed his mace into Slayer's side. Slayer didn't move; his eyes were only half-open. Mr. B threw the mace aside and once again lifted up the blue tektite. The moonlight hit, causing the light to shine on the *Spinosaurus*'s eyes.

Everyone stopped and watched in horror as the fin on the *Spinosaurus*'s back glowed red. It wagged its tail and sent the few dinosaurs watching from the back flying through the air. They had failed; there was no stopping the giant skeleton. Once it got over the wall, the whole city would be doomed.

Dylan watched as the Spinosaurus roared. It was deafening. He ducked as the tail swung by his head. Slayer was still down, but Raspberry had jumped onto the back of the skeleton.

Mr. B raised the blue tektite in the air. "I have brought you back from the dead. Together we can rule the world!" The *Spinosaurus* threw Raspberry off him and turned his snout to Mr. B.

Mr. B must have felt as if he was the winner; he looked so happy that the *Spinosaurus* was following him. Then things took a turn. The *Spinosaurus* pulled one of the *Triceratops* guards, and with his sharp claws, he put him on the ground and stepped on him. There was a squelching noise as the *Spinosaurus* began speaking, "And who asked you to bring me back? I, the great Bob, work alone."

"Bob? Seriously, your name is Bob?" Caleb called out. "You've got crazy names like Slayer and Mr. Big Al, and you come around the biggest and scariest thing here and you're calling yourself Bob? Oh, how terrifying. You better watch out. Bob is coming!"

Dylan felt that Caleb had truly lost his marbles. "What are you doing? Shut up before he eats us!"

Mr. B addressed the *Spinosaurus*. "I have brought you these Neanderthals to snack on so that you can rebuild your strength." If he thought that Bob was going to be impressed by this, he was wrong.

Bob looked down at Caleb and Dylan. "You stupid dinosaur." He turned back to Mr. B. "I have no hunger for humans. Not yet anyway. But as I said, I work alone."

Dylan saw that the entrance to the tunnel was no longer blocked. If they were quick enough, they might be able to get into the tunnel. Bob was way too big to fit into the entrance. But if he saw them running, he might go after them, and with his jaws, he could probably swallow them in one bite. Dylan pointed out the tunnel to Terry. "We have to make a run for it."

Terry took Caleb's hand, "We need for Bob to be distracted." As the words came out of his mouth, there was a loud scream. Bob had closed his jaws down on Mr. B's tail. Bob tossed him fifty feet in the air. Dylan could not take his eyes off Bob as he opened his mouth wide, and Mr. B fell in with a scream. The jaws shut; they could see Bob chewing and swallowing Mr. B.

Slayer had gotten to his feet, and grabbing his sword, he yelled, "We must destroy the beast Bob before his body is fully repaired!"

Dinosaurs from all sides ran at Bob, jumping all around him. "I think that the terrifying Bob is distracted. Maybe we should run now," Caleb said, his voice strong. Dylan grabbed his other hand, and the three of them took off. They had to dodge the giant bone tail that Bob was swinging from side to side.

Dylan noticed that all the dinosaurs were working together now. He saw no sign of Paige, however. Had she run off into the jungle? Or had she died in the battle? They made it to the tunnel.

All three collapsed against the wall. Terry was trying to catch his breath "What do we do now?" he asked.

Dylan was holding his side where Paige had scratched him. "We need to get help. Maybe if we can get to the main entrance, we can call the police."

Caleb rolled his eyes at him. "And say what? That Bob the Spinosaurus has been brought magically back to life by another insane dinosaur and our friends, the other dinosaurs, are fighting him, but they need help?"

Dylan was about to reply when a loud snapping noise got his attention. He grabbed Caleb and Terry and ran further into the tunnel, just as Bob stuck his jaws inside the entrance trying to get at them. The tunnel shook as Bob tried to get in more by slamming his head into the entrance.

Dylan could see that Slayer was attempting to wrestle Bob from the entrance of the tunnel. "Run, get out of here!" Slayer yelled as he stabbed Bob through the rib cage with his sword.

They didn't need to be told twice. They ran down the path. As they went deeper and deeper into the tunnels, the noise of the battle outside muffled. They came to the large room where Dylan had met Slayer. There were paths leading into different tunnels. "Which way will get us close to the gift shop?" Dylan asked aloud. He was hoping Terry had a good knowledge of the park to know the way.

His hopes were dashed when Terry replied, "I don't have a clue."

The sound of nails scraping the tunnel walls filled their ears. "This is the only way to the main entrance," Paige gloated as she sharpened her claws on the rocks. "I am going to enjoy tearing you apart. Which one to start with?"

She moved forward and cornered Caleb. Dylan was not sure what to do. "You lost the battle; Mr. B is dead and he is not coming back. Your friend Bob ate him. You don't have to follow his orders anymore."

Paige turned her snout at him and laughed. "I don't follow anyone's orders. I told you, I like myself for who I am and humans are on the top of my favorite food list. I wonder if Mr. H would make me a pizza out of you. Now, that would be tasty."

Dylan watched as she ran a long black tongue across Caleb's face. "Stop! Let them go, and you can do whatever you want to me." He was trying to think of something quick, but he had no idea what to do. He just wanted to get Caleb out of this. Terry was trying to get his attention; he kept looking up at Dylan. Dylan glanced up, but all he saw was a black, slimy ceiling of tar.

Dylan gave Terry a questioning look; he saw Terry back up against a lever. Dylan looked up again. He understood that was how he had gotten into the tunnel. He had to sink through the tar, but they would not have wanted the tar in the tunnel. The lever must open a hatch to let things through; and Paige was standing right under it.

Dylan nodded to Terry. Now, all he had to do was get Caleb out of the way. "Can I have one last kiss?" he asked Paige. She looked at him and slowly started to change back to human. While she was changing, Terry threw the lever. The tar was slowly coming down.

Paige was fully human again. "Do you still find me beautiful?" She laughed. Dylan no longer felt the same way as he did about her. There were no butterflies in his stomach, only anger. "No, you're just as hideous on the outside as you are on the inside!"

She had a shocked look as Dylan's fist hit her face. He grabbed Caleb by the shirt and pulled him out of the way. Paige was transforming back to a dinosaur when the tar hit her. She fell to the floor; half-human, half-dinosaur, she was stuck. The tar continued to pour.

They could hear her scream. It didn't sound human but not dinosaur either. It was a horrible sound. Terry grabbed Dylan by the arm and jumped. "Let's go," Terry said. They ran up the path; it seemed to take forever, but they finally saw the exit.

Terry was the first to exit the tunnel. He stopped; Dylan and Caleb collided into him. Dylan could see the roaring T-Rex on top of the gift shop. They were just feet away from freedom; the only problem was that the skeletal Bob was standing directly in their path. He roared. Dylan was frozen; not a muscle could move.

It was over; there were no more escapes. Bob lowered his jaws, preparing to eat them whole. Dylan felt a dry, boney tongue on his face. "I'm kinda wishing that Mr. Big would have finished us off, and then we wouldn't have to say that we were eaten by the fearsome Bob," Caleb said. He might have been joking, but he looked terrified.

Dylan watched in horror as the jaws started to close around them. He could see the sharp teeth. They were about to be dinosaur chow. They held onto each other, waiting for the end, but the jaws stopped moving. Bob raised his head; Dylan saw that something was wrong. Bob seemed to be swaying. Suddenly, the bones began to fall to the ground.

Dylan took a deep breath. There was something moving behind where Bob had been standing. The dust from the bones hitting the ground was starting to settle. Dylan was not quite sure what had happened.

"Bonedigger!" Caleb cried. Sure enough, Dylan could see their dog wagging his tail and in his mouth, he was holding the leg bone.

A hand grabbed Dylan; he turned around and was face to face with Slayer. "I think we won," Dylan said. His voice cracked.

XXIX

Dylan's alarm went off Monday morning at normal time. He hadn't gotten much sleep as he and Caleb hadn't gotten home until after 2:00 a.m. He had a hard time explaining what had happened. He finally decided to tell his grandmother that he had found Caleb at Dino Kingdom after he had been lost and hid in the dinosaur's exhibit. Caleb agreed with the story, and their grandmother was so happy to have them both home that she didn't ask too many questions.

As he pulled on his shoes, his grandmother poked her head through the door. "Are you going to go to school today? I told Caleb that he could stay home."

Dylan shook his head. "I'm going to go." His grandmother left. Dylan walked down the hallway and opened Caleb's door. He was still sleeping; Dylan thought that Caleb looked peaceful. He was not sure how long it would take him to be back to his annoying, bratty self. He had gone through a lot.

Shutting the door, he walked away, took his backpack in his hand, and put it on his back. He walked out the front door and was shocked to see the moving truck in Terry's driveway.

Terry approached him. "Hey, how did it go with your grandmother?"

"Not too bad. She was just happy that we were safe," Dylan replied. "Why is there a moving truck in your driveway?"

"My aunt and I are moving into the park. I told her everything that happened. She already knew my secret when she took me in,"

Terry said, scratching his nose. "Slayer is trying to get all the dinosaurs on the same page. I'm going to live there so that I can help out."

Dylan smiled. "I'm going to miss you, man." He extended his hand to shake Terry's.

Terry took his hand. "You are welcome to come visit us anytime."

Dylan nodded; he picked up his bike and began to ride to school. His head was filled with questions. He was going to have to admit to JP that he was right about the school being strange. He thought about the frogman. If he had been the one who put the yearbook in his backpack, how had the principal gotten his bag? What other creatures and mysteries did the school hide?

He made his way to class. As he sat down, he saw the empty desks that had belonged to Terry and Paige. Sam came over to him. "Have a good weekend?" Sam asked.

Dylan took out a notebook and pencil. "It was very bizarre," he said.

JP came in. "Did you guys hear about Paige? The principal said that her family moved away over the weekend." JP sat down. "I wonder if it was because of this stupid report that we had to do."

Dylan rolled his eyes; he had totally forgotten about the report. He opened the notebook to find a note:

> Dylan, I am sorry that I dragged you into my problems. Your mom was my best friend, and you should know that she will always love you. I also figured that you forgot to write the report, so here is mine. Hope we can still be friends.
>
> Terry Dactyl

He turned the page to find a five-page report. He smiled to himself. This school was strange, but he was glad to have friends that would stand with him, no matter how crazy things got.

Don't Miss the Next Bizarre Events at Hellman Elementary!

Payton's birthday is just a couple of weeks away, and he is excited about having his cousin Gabe come to live with his family. However, when Gabe arrives, things take a bizarre turn. Payton doesn't recognize him as the friend he was last year.

Also, Payton's friends are hanging out with Gabe and throwing unusual temper tantrums. Is Payton going crazy? Or is Gabe trying to steal his place in fifth grade? Furthermore, is something more sinister spreading through the hallways?

Find out these answers and more.

The Bizarre Events at Hellman Elementary Book 3

Temper Tantrums Aren't For Fifth Graders!

About the Author

Richard Born grew up in Tennessee. He lived in Memphis until he started high school, when his family moved to Chattanooga. His enthusiasm for writing began in the third grade, and this continued passion was the basis for his high school teachers being forced to place a page limit on his assigned essays. After high school graduation and a year at the University of Tennessee at Chattanooga, Mr. Born made the decision to leave Tennessee to attend Western Kentucky University in Bowling Green. He majored in English, with the area of concentration in creative writing, and minored in film studies. While living in Bowling Green, he also became a foster parent to a number of children. Being a foster parent has given Mr. Born inspiration and insight into writing specifically for children. He has stated that their unique viewpoints on life's daily events—some good, some challenging—are certainly enlightening. He has also said that the children he has been a foster parent to have enriched his life with awareness and purpose of being there for others. He is a firm believer in foster parenting and adoption. Mr. Born has now returned to Tennessee, where he lives with his two sons and a dog named Bandit.

CPSIA information can be obtained
at www.ICGtesting.com
Printed in the USA
LVHW03s0538080918
589426LV00001B/32/P